UNTIL THE END OF THE NINTH

by
Beth Mary Bollinger

Bloomington, IN Milton Keynes, UK

AuthorHouse™
1663 Liberty Drive, Suite 200
Bloomington, IN 47403
www.authorhouse.com
Phone: 1-800-839-8640

AuthorHouse™ *UK Ltd.*
500 Avebury Boulevard
Central Milton Keynes, MK9 2BE
www.authorhouse.co.uk
Phone: 08001974150

First published by AuthorHouse 5/16/2006

ISBN: 1-4259-3665-2 (sc)

Library of Congress Control Number: 2006903885

Printed in the United States of America
Bloomington, Indiana

This book is printed on acid-free paper.

Front cover courtesy of Northwest Museum of Arts and Culture, Spokane, Washington.

Cover design by Kurt Schmierer

Author's photograph by Michele Mokrey.

All unmarked photographs except memorial game program photographs are courtesy of The Spokesman-Review.

from ashes to ashes, life to death, soul to soul
everything is possible in the light of grace

Foreword

There is a Foreword and an Afterword in this novel. One main purpose of the Foreword is to alert the reader to the Afterword (which includes biographies of the players), which I have written so as to give the reader some information about what in this novel is based on fact, what is necessarily fiction, and what is a little in between. It doesn't answer all questions in that regard, but it helps give a sense of the research that went into the book, the interviews that I conducted, the help that I received from historians, survivors, and victims' families, and some details of how I tried to be as faithful to the facts of this tragedy while still presenting a fictionalized account of it.

I know some of you are tempted to flip to the Afterword right now, before reading the novel. I urge you to resist the temptation. Otherwise, a lot of the novel's surprises will be revealed before their time. It would be like peeking at your birthday presents before they were wrapped. Sure, you would enjoy the presents after you opened them. But wouldn't it have been just a little bit more gratifying to be able to wonder at what was in the boxes in the very moment that you were unwrapping them?

The other purpose of the Foreword is to talk a bit about Joan of Arc. You will see in the next few pages that she is the spirit that is referenced on the back cover as having returned to the Earth to help these men. People have asked me, why Joan of Arc? It's an odd question for me, since I can hardly imagine why *not* her, or someone like her (although there's no one like her). Still, I am asked, so here I will try to answer.

Partly it is just the parallels between her story and the story of these men. They all had been in war; they all had been young when they died; they all died by fire; they all died while being true to what they believed to be their destiny; they all were horribly missed by those who loved them; and they all should be remembered forever. Partly, too, it is how she used to comfort the men who lay dying on the battlefield at the end of every day. Whether they were British or French, she comforted them as they died. It was the right thing to do. So if spirits really do come to Earth and help us out in times like this, I believe she would have helped for that reason alone: because it would be the right thing to do, especially when these men had been in a war (World War II), and had fought for their country. Those were the kind of men that she helped in life. They would be the kind of men she would want to help in death. They also were the kind of men who had helped her achieve her own destiny. She would need to try to help them in return.

Some people also have asked me why I chose to describe Joan of Arc's personal story to start each of the five parts of the novel, rather than just to imagine her ethereally. In part it is to emphasize the parallels between her and the 1946 men. In part, however, it is to emphasize the very real and human experience she had that would have drawn her to Spokane at that time in the first place. She *experienced* dying by fire. She *experienced* dying too young, in the passion of youth, when she could not yet know what it meant to fail. She died while living her destiny, while following a calling that came to her from her very cells. That is what these men were doing too. She was human once, as they were. I tell her human story to show that.

It is this novel's combination of the real and the ethereal that opens the door to imagining the possibilities of what happens when people die tragically and unexpectedly, and as a group. For that is what they are: possibilities, not absolutes. Take the unnamed narrator, for example, who can see what is happening, and who knows what everyone is thinking, even without being seen or heard by any of them. The narrator could be anyone – male or female, living or dead – who cares about these men. It is up to you, the reader, to decide (or not to decide, if you choose). In a novel about possibilities, there can be something reassuring about an unidentified narrator.

I do think that imagining the possibility of a feminine spirit coming to help during that tragic time is a way to imagine how the terrible effects of the disaster could have been softened. It honors all the women in the lives of these men to imagine the arrival of that kind of grace.

Spokane, Washington
April 9, 2006

Table of Contents

Preface

There is a seven-foot wide drum in Alaska, built by hand with wetted, then bended, wood, scooped deeply towards the ground. One large bull's skin covers the top – just barely, but it does. The drum stands waist high on tall women, and sits on a wooden stand so that it rests not directly on the ground but in the air. In this way, the sound that comes from it can reach into the empty space that completely surrounds it.

One beat of the drum and every piece of you vibrates, down to the inner marrow of your bones. And while you think you have heard an amazing sound, you have not even heard the half of it. The resonance from this drum is so full and deep that you cannot hear it all. Only the core of the earth can hear every part of this drum's call. One beat of the drum and the ground opens up to sift the sound down into the soil, absorbing every nuance until the earth says yes, yes – I can hear the beat of this drum, I can hear what it is trying to say. And the earth sings back to the drum the echo of its sound – this is what I hear you say, it says to the drum. And this is what I know about what you say; this is what I know, from humanity, from the experience of the world through all of time. Let me give you what I know, the earth says to the drum, and to those who listen to it.

So when you listen to this drum, you hear the echo of the drum's calling. And you hear the earth's own song. This is how you hear this drum. You do not know all of what you hear, or how you hear it. But you feel it in your bones.

And then too, you sense something more than just the earth's song. You sense, too, the whispering, far and away, of angels above, who call to the souls whose songs the earth is singing, as though a prelude is playing, and the curtain is rising, and to the earth they are summoned again, summoned to say, this is what I know about this song.

Perhaps that is why people weep – cry, laugh, weep – when they listen to this drum. For it is through the beat of this drum that they can hear the earth's song. And it is through the beat of this drum that they can know angels gather. And it is through the beat of this drum that they can feel souls return, if just for a moment, to hear and remember and speak of what they know.

Perhaps too, this is how the song of Joan of Arc bubbles up from the earth and down from the sky as it answers the call of the beat of the hearts of The Spokane Nine of 1946. For there is no deeper beat than the beat of the heart.

PART 1

The Prelude

On January 6, 1412, a girl was born in the village of Domremy, France. She was named Jehanne d'Arc (or Joan of Arc, in its anglicized form). It was the Day of the Epiphanies – the Twelfth Night after Jesus' birthday – the day when all things to be known are so known, as they bubble up from below the surface, one image after another.

During Joan's life, the English occupied France. People, including Joan's family and village, suffered terribly from a lack of food, water, stability. Even still, Joan was full of life and kindness. It was a miracle just to have a child like her around when the rest of their world was hard, sad and full of fear.

Even as a child, Joan saw things that others didn't see; understood things that others didn't understand. They say it was Joan who saved the invisible troublemaking faeries that were presumed to live in the town's great Oak tree. It is told that Domremy's priest had informed all the children in the village that the faeries had to go. They caused too much mischief. Their punishment would be banishment, he had told the children.

Joan rose to their defense. That's not fair, she said. They can't help how they act. That's true, the priest replied. Nonetheless, they must go, for they are the ones who are causing the trouble.

But Joan persisted. If God makes everything, then God made the faeries, didn't He? she asked. Yes He did, agreed the priest. And did God make them the way that they are? Yes He did, the priest said. Their very nature? Yes, the priest replied. Well, Joan said, since it is their nature to cause trouble, and since God made them that way, then aren't they only acting in such a way as God wants? And if you banish them, aren't you punishing them just because they're behaving as God wants them to behave? That's not fair, she said again.

The priest laughed. The faeries were allowed to stay.

As she turned a teenager, Joan started hearing the voices of Archangel Michael – the archangel of the warrior – and Saints Catherine and Margaret – the saints for the unfortunate. They told her that it was her destiny to win France back from the English.

Another child could have chosen not to listen. Another child may have chosen fear. But this was not just any child. This was a child who would listen to the voices, and believe in them, even though that meant she left her beloved family and home to follow the sounds of voices that only she could hear.

The voices proved the truth of their words, as Charles VII (the man-to-be-king) appointed her in 1429 as his top general, with generals La Hire and Jean Dunois – the Bastard of Orleans, as he was more fondly known – directly beneath her. They called her the Maid of Orleans when she led them in eight days to lift the siege against that city. It was the warrior within her, and Michael by her side, that led them to victory. And it was during that week, as he watched her save his city from siege, that the Bastard understood that there was something about her. Something different. Something bound for destiny.

The war could have ended there. Would have ended there? Had there not been for the sense that this destiny was not yet fulfilled. That, indeed, it had just begun. And so it was that, later, when the would-be king tried to rein them all in, the Bastard and La Hire went to him and told him he was wrong to stop her. They told him of her skill, her vision, of her physical abilities, her bravery, and of her faith in achieving the impossible. They told him that Joan's gifts were of such magnitude that they had to come from a power greater than herself, and certainly one greater than any of them. She was made for this, the Bastard said. Let her win all of France for you, he said.

So Charles said yes, but really meant no, and gave them the permission they needed to let her follow the voices that she heard. Joan breathed a sigh of relief when she learned she could go on with the battle, even though it meant that she couldn't yet go home, because it did mean that she could finish what she had come there to start. God's will be done, is what she said to anyone who asked. Let God's will be done.

Ferris Field, built in 1936, was considered the best minor league field in the region.

Photo courtesy Northwest Museum of Arts and Culture (L90.182.1)

In the spring of 1946, baseball was born again. World War II was finally over. The boys were finally back. Man after man, boy after boy, each of them was back to play on the field again. It was as though life could begin for the very first time, as though the war could be placed in the past. And while everyday supplies were short, memories were long, and each of them knew there was something magical in the antics of the game that could bring them back to themselves.

So many men sought the field that there was, in fact, a deluge of players. Some were destined for stardom. Others played more on prayer. Some who were ready for the Big Leagues were relegated instead to the minors, bumped by their youth as older prospects back from the war were re-signed. During the war, while the major leagues had continued play, most minor leagues had shut down. Suddenly they were back up and running, with a plethora of players to run with. And for all the players – or almost all – this is what they lived for, had waited for. This was a part of their destiny. To live in a country that went to war. To love those they loved. And to play ball.

Communities in 1946 loved minor league ball. It was before the proliferation of television, so that major leaguers had not yet stolen that kind of daily loyalty that belongs to the home team. And in the still-somewhat-wild West, where the major leagues had not yet migrated, the local minor league teams did well. For even though there were teams that played like the Big Leagues – like the Oakland "Oaks" and the Seattle Rainiers – they weren't absorbed into the major leagues yet, and they still were hundreds of miles away from many communities. So small towns loved minor league ball, and loved their local players like they would love a hero coming to save the day. Newspapers made sure of it, as they wrote the stories that put townsfolk on the edge of a spring full of hope.

Spokane, Washington, was such a town, and The Spokesman-Review was such a paper. On the opposite side of the state from Seattle, Spokane was a small town's small town – the hub of its locale, a river running through it, mountains in the distance, with the wilderness of Canada just to its north. It was a town that was truly at the center of its own universe, dedicated to its way of life, and anxious to see baseball begin.

The town was particularly eager to come back to its modern Ferris Field – nearly a decade old in actual years, but only scarcely used for four years before baseball ended and war began. Baseball just had a way of feeling bigger out at Ferris Field, is what the townsfolk said amongst themselves. At least that's what I heard them say. Everyone agreed that the still-fresh field was an improvement over Old Nat Park, which had gone into disarray, as baseball gradually left there in the years before Ferris Field arrived. Baseball was so long gone at Nat Park that firemen burned down the grandstand there as a field exercise on December 15th that past winter, just 10 days before Christmas and 22 days before January 6th – the Day of Epiphanies – when all that must be revealed can be revealed in a to-the-surface sort of way. And after they demolished the grandstand, they cooked marshmallows over the embering coals. It was quite a sight to see.

I did hear some say that they still missed that old baseball field, which sat in an amusement park on the edge of the river, miles downstream from the center of town and from its waterfall where tribes gathered after the harvest. Old Nat Park may have had its bumps and scars, but it carried with it a legacy of birth, since Spokane had become Spokane just about the time that baseball had arrived and had found its way to the edge of town and to the river rushing beneath it.

It seemed to me that some felt it was abandonment to leave the park behind like they had done when Ferris Field was built. But then I heard others point to modernity, a move away from the years when Old Nat Park had been a place for those who played the game as pros. And then, as consolation, they would, here and there, nod their heads knowingly and remind the nostalgics of Nat Park's *other* legacy. *That* was a legacy to leave behind, they would say, to comfort their comrades who held to old ways.

And it was true, that it would be best to escape that other legacy. For the fire station exercise wasn't the first time those stands had burned. Two Fourths of July – one right before the century mark, one right after it – had also resulted in immolated stands. The second time, in 1906, the fire happened so fast that they say the players barely escaped, were saved only because one of the managers had chased his way back under the stands to the dressing rooms, searing his hands along the way, just to warn them they had to get out. With or without clothes on: get out now. Hard to forget *that* legacy.

I heard a few people, usually the nostalgics, say that the fires at Old Nat Park had just been baseball's way of sympathizing with Spokane's own penchant for burning down, which it had done back in 1889, when its name had been Spokane Falls, and in the summer, when baseball players play. And now that Spokane and baseball were both here to stay, well – it wouldn't, couldn't happen again. But then others said that fire was the park's curse, not worth the risk such fires likely cause. Still others just rolled their eyes and patiently explained how fires just happened to be the natural fate for wooden stands, how summer just happened to be the time that fires occurred, and how the Fourth of July just happened to be the summer holiday that brings together that always potentially dangerous combination of careless young boys and firecrackers.

Whichever way, we all knew that the firefighters' exercise at Old Nat Park – in December, not July – had burned that grandstand down for the last time. And what was left, miles away, and not near the river at all, was the town's beautiful, smooth, modern Ferris Field. It was on that field that we impatiently waited for the season to begin.

And so it was that, by March of 1946, a month before the season's opening night, nearly every morning's sports section carried some sort of update on the home team – the Spokane Indians. The Tribe. The Spokane Nine.

For that is what the newspaper called them. The Spokane Nine. There was nothing special in the name. They called a Tacoma basketball team the "Tacoma Five," a Hawaii football team the "Hawaiian Eleven." It didn't matter that the nine, or five, or eleven was technically an incorrect number, given how substitute players raised any team's number higher than the minimum needed for the sport in question. It was just the way they wrote headlines then.

And calling this team "The Tribe" made sense. Just like the Cleveland Indians, only with a serious "S" on their chests, to represent "Spokane," a real Indian tribe located in and around the same-named city. Not starkly in the middle of their chests, like Superman, but off to the side (humbly, perhaps) – though most of us could have sworn that the players *were* Supermen, regardless of where the "S" was sewn on the shirt.

And sometimes the paper called them the "Spokanes," after the tribe itself. This made "The Spokane Nine" a little more special than other numbered names, since Spokane was the city but also the tribe, and if you called them the Spokane Nine you were, in a way, calling them the Indians.

And sometimes they called them "nine boys" too – an affectionate, almost possessive term, even if the word "possess" is too optimistic. Really, can one ever possess nine boys? Isn't it just a lot more likely that any group of boys that grows to nine or more is out of the reach of any kind of centralized control?

Spokane called them the boys. Just that – the boys. We did love them so.

The Spokesman-Review reported on how the nation would be loving baseball that year. "1946 BEST YEAR IN BIG BASEBALL," the headline read on April 14th. "Hustling Is Keyword," read a subheadline. "After four wartime seasons, major league baseball returns to peace-time caliber with scores of great stars resuming their careers...."

The Spokesman reported on baseball's controversies, too. "CITY LAW BARS NEGRO PLAYERS" was a headline for an article out of Jacksonville, Florida. "Jackie Robinson, John Wright to Miss Game," read the subheadline. It would be another year before the Brooklyn Dodgers would put Jackie Robinson in their line-up as the first Black man in the 20th century in a major league game. But even as a minor leaguer, his presence created consternation. "Montreal can bring Second Baseman Robinson or any other Negro player to Jacksonville, Miss., they wish, but they can't go on the field."

The paper also reported on upcoming hopes, also courtesy of the Dodgers. The first-ever "Brooklyn Against The World" series was announced for high school stand-outs. Around the country, the Dodgers teamed up with local papers like The Spokesman to spon-sor all-star games around the country for the best of each region's youth, with one boy from each location to be sent to Brooklyn at summer's end for an all-star game against the best of Brooklyn youth. Spokane's all-star game was set for July 10th. "Stay tuned," was the paper's motto. This, it implied, would be the greatest spring ever.

Other things happened too that spring, besides baseball. And The Spokesman-Review duly reported them. "TRIBUNAL HEARS ROSENBURG RANT," read one headline on April 16th. "Nazi Ex-pounds Ideology After Slaughter Testimony," was the subheadline. "JAP WHO ORDERED BATAAN DEATH MARCH DIES LASHED TO POST," was another headline on April 3rd. "Gen. Homma Wears Hood as Bullets Thud Home in Patch on Heart," came the details – a war-sanctioned execution for the man whose own orders had killed thousands of American and Filipino war prisoners.

Reports included the personal. "JILTED VETERAN ENDS HIS LIFE" came one report. He died in Boise, so many miles from Spo-kane that it was not a hometown story. His newsworthiness must have lain in his broken heart. "The man told police he had been 'left' by a woman but gave no details, shortly before he died," the article said. He had survived four Mediterranean campaigns just in time to come home and pop a handful of strychnine tablets. Better to have dirt dumped on your coffin than kicked in your face, he must have thought.

But even with national and international news to report, both on and off the baseball field, The Spokesman-Review knew the importance of helping its readers return to peacetime rituals. There was something about reminding Spokane that life could be normal, if we let it. Someday, it could return to that. And between the special events and a regular ball schedule, baseball could be – should be – one of those rituals, in a stalwart way. Someday the outcome would have that sort of peace.

And so The Spokesman's litanies included near-daily reports on the home team, even in those preseason weeks.

One of the first articles was a story on Levi McCormack, a Nez Perce Indian and the Spokane Indians' left fielder since before the war. The article spilled over with excitement that "the Chief" would be back in action. The article reminisced about the late 1930s and early 1940s, when Levi had played before. "The likable Indian was a favorite with Spokane fans because of his continuous hustling on the field, his speed, throwing arm and great defensive ability," the newspaper said. And what an outfield: "with McCormack in left, Dwight Aden in center and Pete Hughes in right field, [it] was considered to be the finest in the northwest," the paper remembered in a near sigh.

I knew that Levi was glad to remember as he read the article and thought about the past. And why wouldn't he be? They had been the three in charge of that outfield that last year, as the Tribe had baptized Ferris Field back then when it was brand new. It had been a special place to play, especially in those first years. No more hitting balls into the Spokane River was the joke, since balls hit over the left field fence at Old Nat Park looked as though they would splash into the river that rushed by just below.

Though Levi would have liked to have played at Nat Park. There were places to picnic, a beautiful carousel, a swimming pool.... But more than that, it was near the river. The teams back then may have lost balls now and again over the fence and towards the river. But when he thought about the river, as he thought about the park, I felt him remember those players he had watched. I felt him think of Babe Ruth, who had hit a homerun out of that very park when Levi had been about 11. Everyone came for that game – the military men stood on the sloping bank across the way, and boys hung from the left field fence. It felt like Levi had been there that day in 1924 (as he stood now in 1946, reading the newspaper about his return). I could almost see him, sitting on that left field fence, or on a bridge between the military and the game (if there had been a bridge there). Too poor to buy tickets. Too much of a boy loving baseball to stay away.

Those were great days for baseball, back when Levi was young. And playing in that park, by the river, would have been quite a legacy to join. It could tell it was how he felt about it. It made sense, to feel that way.

Thinking about Old Nat Park wasn't just nostalgic for Levi though. It was real too. Sometimes, before the war (and I knew this, or felt it to be true), Levi had gone out to that park to sit and imagine how it would feel to hit a ball so hard that it actually landed in the river, 80 feet beyond the fence.

Well, and of course he would have gone to the park. Everyone went to Nat Park. It had a swimming pool. A dance hall. People came with hats on, all dressed up on Sunday afternoons. But for Levi, there was more. It was as though I saw him now as he was back then – wandering away from the dance hall to the grandstand. Even bringing a bat and ball now and then to try it out, and watch balls fly over the outfield wall.

Still, old park or no, river or no, when Levi and Dwight and Petey had taken over at the new Ferris Field back in those years before the war, and with all the play of all the others, the Tribe had brought in the crowds. And won the pennant by 18 games in 1941.

And then the war.

It was easy to see why Levi had come back to baseball. Playing ball was what he did. It was harder to know why he had come back to Spokane. Just that he was coming back to what he knew, I think. And that he knew he would get to play here. Which is what he had to do, it seemed. Play ball, that is.

He wouldn't be back out at Old Nat Park to practice though, since the firefighters had burned down the stands and then cooked marshmallows over the embering remains. Ferris Field, on the other hand – that was a place that would last through the ages. Levi pondered the article about him as he got ready for the newer field's newest baptism, now that the war was over and he was back with the team.

Then all of a sudden, I saw that he *would* go back out to Nat Park at some point, to where the Indians used to play. And I saw that, when he did, he would hit a ball or two out into the river. He would skip the fence this time. Just hit it straight into the current.

What nobody knew, not for sure, was how many breakfast tables at homes across Spokane were full of people full of excitement at the news of Levi's return, and how many children were grinning at the thought of getting to watch the "Chief" run bases again. "He's the best player *ever*," I heard one boy say to his father just before he went out in the backyard in a red shirt – just like Levi – and hit balls into the fence. If he worked at it, Dad said, maybe he'd play for the Indians one day, like the Chief. But would he be as tall and strong? was what I heard the boy think. He could only hope.

In the end, it was unanimous. Levi's return was what both the team and Spokane needed to carry forward as minor league ball began. As if the team and town would be lost without him playing in this game that they had lost to the war for too long. As if "The Chief" embodied the very nature of the team. And why not? They were, after all, the Indians by name, as he was by blood. And he was, after all, the very kind of fellow that the town could embrace – strong, both physically and mentally, unavoidably noticeable with his height and handsome looks, happy to take the praise yet a little unassuming, too, as though his physique and talent were just gifts of life over which he had no control. In the end, a story about Levi McCormack meant a story about how the town could hope for the best.

Other stories were of less magnitude. It seemed that no story was too miniscule.

"INDIANS' OWNER HEADING SOUTH" was one headline. "Owner Sam Collins and Mrs. Collins left by car this morning for California," the newspaper reported. Collins, a retired business-man and the Indians' brand new owner, was headed to meet up with Glenn Wright, a past major leaguer and the Indians' brand new manager, down at their spring training camp, where they would "prepare for the invasion of 27 players."

I went there to see for myself how spring training would go. I saw men standing around as they collected at the practice field. Some knew each other from seasons past, but most everyone was new to the team, and to each other. They were awkward in their greetings as they eyed each other up and down, wondering who would play where, who would win the starting spots, knowing that at least some of them were playing for the Indians rather than a bigger team like Casey Stengel's Oakland "Oaks" only because the bigger teams already had too many players returning from war.

And then there was Levi – implacable yet with kind eyes too, looking from face to face when no one was looking, seeing beyond the face to the spirit within.

It was Levi who took the steps that moved the group to settle in. After watching their faces and seeing their ways, he walked around in his signature red shirt, introducing himself to this one or that one, mostly shaking hands and finding out where they came from, creating small spaces of common ground. In that way, awkward talk turned to warm-up play, which turned to time for supper. With most just back from war, it was turning out they had more in common than baseball and the Wild West.

The news in the paper included those players who rejected the team. The headlines reported that one of the best and brightest catchers had turned down the Indians and a bonus check of $800 because a California team was offering bonuses of $100 more than any other team's best offer. "At least Sam tried" was the quote from the team.

And then it was back to the miniscule details of nothing-much-at-all.

The soft news had its blessings, for the fun was in the detail:

> TRIBE BOTHERED BY WILD RUNNING: It seems that the training sessions have put the lads on edge....
>
> Said Wright: "I am going to have to invent a method of slowing some of these guys down – particularly Outfielder Bob James – the wild man from Arizona. Against Stockton in the first [exhibition] game last week-end he drove in all but two of the runs – they scored on wild pitches – as we won 7 to 6. But he went crazy on the base paths. One of his feats was to rap the apple against the right field fence and then slide head first into second only to find that Bob Paterson, center fielder, was still roosting there.

"In the next time at bat he clouted to the center boards and a 10-foot concrete wall couldn't have stopped him at second. He was tossed out at third by 10 feet. I asked him if it wasn't customary to watch the third base coacher, and he apologized by saying that it had been so long since he had been on the sacks that he guessed he had just gone crazy.

"But," said Wright, and he appeared pleased over it, "I guess I can find ways of stopping him at second if he will just continue to powder that ball against the outfield fences."

I sat with Bob James as he laughed at the article. He knew he had gotten in his own way that game, and felt glad that Wright had turned it around to make it look like he had done well. I watched as he shrugged off his new teammates' jokes about it all. Mostly he looked the other way, towards the outfield and the homerun fence. But I knew that he felt good when Wright came up, thumped him on the back, and said, "Nice job, Wild Man." And once, when no one was looking but me, Bob picked up the paper and read the article slowly, then stuffed it in his bag for when his brother came to visit.

Also within the detail of the articles was the uncertainty of who would end up on the team. Names came and went; players listed as promising would suddenly drop off that list, with some even choosing to quit baseball altogether, going home to be with families instead. Even more than before the war, minor league teams were trying to corral a troupe of moving targets, and Spokane was no exception.

Added to the uncertainty was whether they would end up with a decent catcher in the backstop. The paper tried to be optimistic but the truth was that Wright wasn't happy with their starting catcher, and the backup, a utility player named Mel Cole, was injured.

He was in pain with each throw. I could hear him think his way through that pain. Grit teeth – throw – don't let it show, Mel Cole thought on each throw. It wasn't so bad when he batted. Or when he caught. It was the throw. To the mound. To the mound. To second. To the mound. It wore him out. Sometimes, it wore him out too much.

"Whas wrong with ya?" The manager snapped at him. Wright had been drinking again. It was a new development for the team, and not a good one. "I'll be fine," Mel answered casually. I'm fine, I heard him think, as he willed it to be true. Make it fine, I heard him pray to a God in whom he believed. It seemed that Wright was just looking for an excuse to boot him. Mel didn't like the drink, for sure, at least not the way Wright drank, or when, and Wright knew it. It didn't help that Wright could blame Mel's lack of play on this injury. Mel turned back to his job. Grit teeth. Throw. Don't. Let. It. Show.

And what *about* pitchers? "INDIANS STRONG DOWN MIDDLE BUT WEAK IN PITCHER'S BOX" came one headline. "If your pitching is bad, all a good defense will do is hold the score down," the article warned. The pitching was so bad, all the bats broke, according to another article:

> You can see why Manager Glenn Wright is worrying about a pitching staff.... The pitching in the Spokane Indian camp has been [so] poor [that] batters have been breaking bats right and left and the Indians are running out of ash.
>
> Tuesday night Manager Wright wired the home office in Spokane to rush two dozen war clubs here as soon as possible. He said the initial two dozen with which the camp started had dwindled at the rate of four a day by the kindling route. This meant that when the lads lined up Thursday morning for batting practice there were four hale and hearty baseball bats in circulation....

"He was drunk," Denny Spellecy said to his fellow newsmen at The Spokesman after listening to Wright's slurs. But Denny had held his tongue and let Wright talk. He had caught him in the middle of a binge, while Wright was still funny and mostly coherent, coming up with quotes for the next day's paper. Besides, Denny would need Wright's help as they got Spokane ready for the Dodgers' all-star game for local high schoolers. The paper was a sponsor and Denny was in charge. "No reason to judge a man a couple of bad nights," he said, as he secretly hoped that was all it would be.

The newspaper also told of how the city was so anticipating a love for the 1946 team that ticket sales were better than they ever had been. "83 percent of the box seats already are sold," the paper reported on April 18th. "Previously the best record was in 1939, when 26 per cent of the box seats were gone on the day the season opened."

There was a story of the beloved pre-war center fielder Dwight Aden, Levi's outfield mate and now the team's business manager. "There is little sense in telling Spokane baseball fans much about the baseball record of Dwight Aden," the article said:

> Because, young or old, they can and will tell you about the greatest outfielder Spokane had cavorting in center field for many years.... Probably the greatest thing that can be said about "D.A." besides being known as a "ball player's ball player," is that he dropped only one fly ball in all the time he played baseball either in college or in the professional ranks. And that little miscue was one that made everyone present the fateful night blink, then gasp, and finally start mumbling, "It couldn't have happened...."

The article then talked about the details of Dwight's business manager job and how well he was doing it. It ended, though, on a wistful note:

> [Dwight Aden] will tell you he is glad to be out of the playing department of baseball, but one gets the idea that he only half means it. Take a good look at him if he slows down enough on opening night and see if he has that faraway look. Five will get you ten it will be there and the same bet goes for the many fans who will miss seeing that familiar bolt of lightning race to the far corners and haul down a line drive to save another Spokane pitcher some trouble.

Dwight smiled as he read. He laughed at the part about a "faraway look" and then put down the paper and rushed to ensure that bats got to camp by bus. As if he had *time* to be nostalgic, he thought, and got ready to go back to his insurance sales job. But then he paused. He was thinking of opening night. He paused a moment longer. I wondered how it would feel for him, when he wasn't playing ball on opening night.

Another article talked about Dwight Aden's replacement, Bob Paterson. It spoke of how the outfield was "gelled" now, with Paterson – a casualty of the Oakland Oaks' spillover – in center, "Levi (Chief) McCormack" in left, and Bob James in right. It noted that Paterson was "listed as the fastest man on the squad and an outstanding ball hawk." But then it warned:

> He'll have to be, to make Spokane fans forget his predecessor, Dwight Aden, who is now the club's business manager. Aden played here from 1938 through 1942 and in all that time only committed one error.

Back at training camp, I sat with Bob Paterson as he read the article. He frowned as he read. There was no other story for him than that he was there to replace Dwight Aden. He had heard it before. He would hear it again. I knew he was tired of it.

"Don't think about it," Levi told him. (When had Levi noticed he was worried?) "If you think about it, you'll have trouble. No one wants that. Besides, they got you down as the fastest man. And a ball hawk. Just be that. That's all you need to be."

Levi did not often lecture other players about their game, especially when he wasn't asked. But he was only saying what needed to be said, and he knew he was the right one to say it, knowing Dwight as he did, seeing Bob's worry as he could. I knew Bob appreciated Levi's words. Even still, Bob kept focusing on the article, and I could feel the pressure he felt to replace the "best ever." He ran a couple of laps to take his mind off it all. Fastest man, fastest man, cycled through his steps as he ran. At least *something* was his, he thought, as he broke into a sprint.

Yes, 1946 was to be a banner, banner year for Spokane ball.

And all of it culminated on April 26th – the long-awaited season opener.

A lot happened on the eve of that opener. There was the unveiling of the home uniforms – quietly white with black trim and caps. There was a ticker tape parade – across Sprague Avenue, up to Riverside, down to Madison. There was the announcement of a special luncheon for the entire team by the Lions Club, and another that the Tribe would be practicing that evening. Come take a look at your team, the newspaper urged.

And then there was a firing before the luncheon. From a hospital bed.

It started when they couldn't find the manager.

"Where's Wright?" the owner had growled. None of them would say – and it wasn't my place to say it for them. (Not that I could have. Not that they saw me, or could hear me, or even feel my presence, even if I wanted them to.) "Where is he?" Sam said again, looking at Dwight.

"No one's seen him," Dwight said, as he had been saying all day. There was no need to add anything about whether it was a drinking binge. Sam already knew. He had been the one to discover Wright missing, when calls to California had gone unanswered.

Sam sighed. He had no time for this as he lay on his hospital bed, still recovering from week-old surgery. It was fair that he wanted to depend on Wright as a man who knew the game – not the inside of every bar.

"I'd say Mel Cole," Dwight said again. "He's got it, Sam. It's in him. He plays with that injury and never says a word. He knows the game. He can make this work."

Sam nodded. They had been using Mel to coach the younger pitchers. It was only logical to use him to manage the whole team. Besides, there wasn't anyone else. Dwight couldn't – he already was doing too much, between managing the team's business affairs and his insurance sales job. "Go get Cole," Sam said.

"INDIANS CHANGE MANAGERS ON EVE OF SEASON – COLLINS NAMES MEL COLE," read the headline. "Wright Release Comes As Shock – Failing Health Is Reason." As if embarrassed by their clear shock at the change, the newspaper hastened to add that Mel is a "likeable catching veteran ..." Still, the words implied: he's only 25. It's the day before the opener. What could this new owner be thinking?

There were rumors that Cole was temporary – chosen because his injury would end up sidelining him anyway. The article emphasized that a permanent manager, one with credentials, would be chosen soon.

The newspaper's impression was how Sam presented it to Mel Cole. "Just hold down the fort, Mel," Sam said. "We just need you for a short time, until we get someone – well, else. More experienced."

Mel listened. Pondered the words. He had talked to Dwight already, who had told him it would be his team, if he wanted it to be. And though Dwight had known no such thing, Mel had believed him anyway. Which was better than not believing.

When Dwight and Mel had talked, I could feel that Mel was hardly breathing, he was so nervous. Both Dwight and I knew Mel wanted to coach someday. "But already?" Mel had asked. So Dwight had coached him on coaching – told him how Mel knew best, since he'd been at training camp, watching the play. No one knows better than you right now, Dwight had said. He'd given Mel something to think about. "No one knows better than you right now," Dwight had said again, seeing in the young man a good match with the new owner. Mel was quiet, calm. He would listen to Sam. Would Sam listen to Mel?

And now, as Mel met with the owner, with Sam telling him just to "hold down the fort," but with Mel knowing that his time was now, if he wanted ... knowing Dwight was right – that he *was* the one who knew the team, right now ... remembering what his wife Mimi had said when he had told her of the possibility of getting the head job – "they'd be lucky to have you," she'd said ... knowing that he didn't have Glenn Wright's experience, not nearly, but also knowing how much he cared about the game, and these men, and knowing he could help the men on the team, wherever their abilities stood at any moment in time ...

Knowing all that, knowing now or never, Mel Cole, that "likeable catching veteran" just hours away from the opening pitch, swallowed. "I'm thinking we need to make some changes, Mr. Collins," he said.

"Changes?" Sam said.

"Changes to tonight's lineup," Mel said.

Sam cocked his head to the side, crossed his arms and leaned back in his hospital bed. "Just what sort of changes were you thinking about, Mel?"

"The infield ..." Mel began.

Sam interrupted, holding up his hand and shaking his head no. "I told you already – Sunseri is out at first. Gone. But we've got that first baseman from the Oaks. Just in time. Just a kid, but one of their best. Vic Picetti. Stengel shoulda kept him closer, is what Dwight thinks. A stroke of luck for us. The other positions – they're set. Changes now would just get in the way. As for pitching – it's Kinnaman. Bob's already got experience with this team. He should pitch tonight, for old times' sake, if nothing else." Sam shrugged, as though there was nothing left to resolve.

Mel shrugged back. "Kinnaman shouldn't start," he said, letting go of his infield comment but holding on to his pitcher change, willing his eyes to stay fixed on the owner.

Sam shook his head no. "Kinnaman's fine. More than fine. He knows this team, played a helluva season in 1941 – he won 22 games that season, Mel." Then Sam stopped and looked more closely at Mel's steady gaze. "So who would you say instead?" he asked.

"Milt Cadinha," Mel said. "I know he just got here a week ago. But Bob Kinnaman just got here last night. Says his arm's not ready. Besides, the *team* may know Bob, but the players don't. Milt – he's got the throws right now. I re-checked his record in Tacoma from before the war. He's real steady, Mr. Collins. When he pitches to me, too."

"You checked on his record?" Sam asked, surprised.

Mel nodded. "I knew him from then. And I thought, if I was going to be manager, I should be checkin' stats," he said, a little embarrassed.

Sam kept looking at Mel. Then he nodded. "Put Cadinha on the mound, if you think he'll be best for tonight." He paused. "Seems like you're taking this job seriously, son. I appreciate that. And it *is* your team to manage right now. You decide. Just don't get carried away. Check with us first," he said, not unkindly.

Mel nodded. That's what Dwight had said, too.

"Oh, and Mel?" Sam said. "Enough 'Mr. Collins.' You need to call me Sam." They shook hands then.

And so it was that, credentialed or not, right from the beginning Mel Cole intended to take his job seriously. Suddenly there were changes for opening night that Spokane didn't understand. The starting pitcher was changed; the first baseman was changed.... When Mel Cole, that "likeable young man," all of 25 years old, took over, well – he took over. And they won that first game 5-0, in front of an ever-adaptable throng of fans, shown by a photo so newsworthy that it found its way to the paper's front page the next day. That pitcher, Milt Cadinha – what a game he pitched. And Bob Paterson, that young center fielder who had Dwight Aden's "big shoes to fill," was a standout too. "Paterson Provides Indians' Power," one caption read. So did the "Chief" – the fans' favorite – as he ducked a tag-out between first and second long enough to give the fleet-footed Paterson time to score one of their runs.

Not that there was any doubt at any point as to who would win that game. The Indians got out ahead right up front and stayed that way through to the end. Still, Levi's baserunning gave the fans something to cheer about, as they watched their favorite player help out their most-watched newcomer on that first night of the 1946 season.

After the game, after everyone was gone, underneath the stadium shadows and in the pale, pale light of the waning moon, Levi walked back out onto the field, scooped up a palmful of dirt from the shoeprints between first and second base, sifted the dirt between his hands as though he were washing them with it, dusted them off until nary a speck of dirt remained, and then smoothed his hands across his forehead and streaked two fingers from each hand across his cheeks out to the sides of his face.

Then he tilted his face towards the sliver of the moon and drank in its light before turning to walk off the field, knowing he would return.

More happened after the season opener. There was the disastrous landslide of losses in the first road trip; the steadying, follow-up energy that brought more wins than losses; the momentary first-place toehold during another away trip; the second chance to beat the team that had pounded them so soundly early on; the success at that second chance, by just a whisker of an edge; the spirits flying high on the heels of that success, which could only help on the very next day, for yet another on-the-road trip....

And that would be "all she wrote," as the expression goes. A strong team in a great year, illuminating two or three stars to be moved on into the Big Leagues.

Except for one thing.

In the midst of this season, in the midst of the camaraderie, in the midst of a love for the game – something happened.

There's a book by Joseph Heller entitled "Something Happened." Once someone I know started reading it but couldn't finish. Her sister had read it though, and told her to keep reading. "Why?" she wanted to know. "Because in the end, something happens," her sister said.

So my friend tried again. And still couldn't quite get through it. Maybe she was too young to appreciate the life of a narrator many years older than she was. Maybe she was too different from the narrator to stay engaged with the story of his life. Whatever the reason, she compromised. She gave up reading the in-between pages and went straight to the end.

Her sister was right. Something indeed happened. It stunned her, so strongly did something happen.

Sometimes you live your life without paying attention to anything other than what sits right in front of you. And then something happens in such a way that everything is changed forever. Sometimes it happens just to one person. Sometimes it happens to a group. Sometimes it happens to a whole team of men.

In 1946, that kind of something happened to the Spokane Nine.

PART 2

Jesus Wept

Joan was a general like no other. She held no fear, and it always worked. She never doubted she would win. And yet even as she won, she was always the first to inspect the field after a day's battle, looking for the wounded, French and English alike, seeking medical help for those who would live, giving comfort to those who would not. One of the soldiers asked her why she did not leave that work to the medics. She looked at him as though his question made no sense. It's the right thing to do, she finally said.

One day, the voices told her that she would be wounded by noon. She told her friend Katherine, who begged her to miss the battle. It's just one day, Katherine said. But Joan shook her head no. How can I ask these men to fight if I am afraid for my own safety? she said. So she led the morning's charge until she fell from her steed with an arrow in her shoulder. She was crying in pain, and the Bastard went to retreat the troops. But she stopped him, and told him through her tears to break off the arrow's shaft instead and to place her back on her horse, so she could continue the battle and show the men that their effort was not for naught, that she would stay by their side even as she bled. Victory was had that day. By the next, they had won all of what they had come to win.

There is another story, a legend of sorts, that the French soldiers captured one of their own who had deserted the army – a man they called the Dwarf because of his immense size. They were angry at his desertion. Yet they were able to capture him only because he had returned! Joan stopped his execution to hear his defense. The Dwarf told her he had deserted the troops because he had gone home to try to save his wife from an English invasion of their small village. But he had been too late. She already had been killed. I came back because I had nowhere else to go, he said. I will serve you to my death, if you let me. You are always welcomed here, Joan said. You are France, he said.

On May 24, 1430, a little more than a year after her great victory in Orleans, with the war still raging and her efforts restricted by Charles, Joan of Arc was captured in battle. She was trapped in a castle with no way out. The Dwarf died at her feet as he tried to save her. In that way, he did as he had promised. He served her until his death.

Her captors, French citizens, offered her up to the French first. But Charles only feigned interest. Finally Joan's captors gave up and sold her to the British instead. The Brits brought her to Rouen, France, and gave her to Catholic Bishop Pierre Cauchon with the *understanding that he would prosecute her ecclesiastically as a heretic.*

Trial began on February 21, 1431. Under the guise of the Pope's authority, and with a half-promise from the British of becoming an Archbishop if he succeeded, Bishop Cauchon gathered a hand-picked jury of priests, levied no specific charges against her, and forced her to defend herself without legal assistance. In the months following, under Cauchon's direction, the priests threatened her with death by fire if she did not recant all of what she said that she had done in the name of God. They refused to administer the blessed Sacrament to her. They falsified a letter from Charles encouraging her to trust them. They did what they could to convince her to give up and confess.

The first trial failed. The second trial ended on May 24, 1431, when Joan put her mark on a piece of paper that denounced, among other things, the voices of Michael, Catherine and Margaret that she had heard telling her of her destiny to win France.

On May 28, 1431, she recanted this recantation. In that moment, she publicly reclaimed the trio of voices and the destiny that had brought her to these trials in the first place. It would not be for naught, all that she had done. Instead it was her destiny. She claimed it. She knew it. She was right to do as she did. Now she would die.

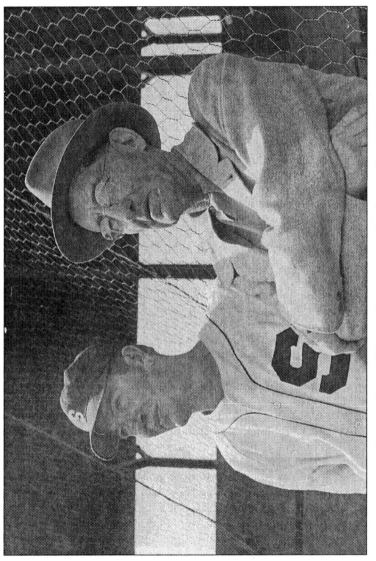

Owner Sam Collins and manager Mel Cole stand together as they watch the Spokane Indians play ball.

Photo courtesy Dwight Aden, Sr.

May 16, 1946: Headline: "INDIANS STOP NEAR SHUTOUT"
Subheadline: "Tie Victoria In Ninth; Win In Twelfth"

To the Victor goes the Victoria. Or so it seemed on May 15, 1946, the day the game was played. Nine was the lucky number – "in the Ninth," the key phrase. Winning was the ultimate result. In extra innings, no less. It was in the ninth that they tied Victoria. It took more than nine to produce the win. They needed three more innings that day to get the win. They needed 12 to win.

If they hadn't put it all together in the ninth, they would have been shut out. Silenced for the day. All that effort, all that batting, all that work, all for naught.

The Indians were lucky to beat Victoria that night. It took a lot, to beat Victoria like that. More than perseverance, more than hope – faith too, and maybe a commitment to the mundane. Always a commitment to the mundane. Playing day in, day out, game after game, pitch after pitch – and then, in a moment's silence, when all seems statically standstill, someone does something to change the flow, or create it.

On May 15, 1946, one or more Indians did something in the ninth. Or so the next-day headline said. Though it didn't say what. The article failed to say who hit when, who was on base, who crossed home plate for the Indians to tie up the score in the top of the ninth. All the article said is how Victoria's pitcher must have felt. "It was a heartbreaker for Hurler Bob Jensen," the pitcher for Victoria (the pitcher for victory) "to lose as he pitched shutout ball for eight and two-thirds innings...." It broke the heart of the hurler for victory to have the Indians raise their capacity at literally the last moment, only one more out to go, and make something happen. Their last best chance. And not for naught.

So what is the consequence when you tie victory in the ninth, and then have the audacity to surge on beyond it, going all the way to the twelfth to beat victory itself? Is it transcendence? Or is it a foolhardy version of Russian roulette? Perhaps it depends on the way you do it. Do you play as a team? The team that plays together ...

They had become a close bunch, the articles had been telling Spokane. Individuals had welded together. Vic Picetti, the first baseman who had gotten the nod at the last minute on opening night, had turned into one of their best and brightest prospects. He was also the youngest, almost the only one not just back from the war. "The Kid," they called him. And even with the fluidity of the minor leagues (where one day you're playing next to your best friend and the next day he's gone on to the Big Leagues), and even with just 20 days into the season, the Indians had figured out how to be close.

Maybe they could get close like that because they had already hit their slump and were on a precarious but possible rise, so that every win was icing on the cake. Or maybe it was because they were "The Tribe" – being the Indians and all – so that they were just supposed to gel as a clan. Or maybe it was because they had started winning in the ninth – like they did that day against Victoria – which was their way of showing that they could pull games out of the fire at just the last minute. And really, maybe they got close because of that ability to win against all odds. It has a way of bringing a team together.

Or maybe it was more than even all that. Maybe it was the year, too. For 1946 was the first season after the war, after minor leagues had shut down, after they had all come back to life as they had known it. And maybe it was the war that had given them practice in the first place on how to appreciate what stands right before you (where one day you're in the trenches next to your best friend and the next day he's gone, only not to a place where you can call him up to talk). Maybe the war had taught them how to appreciate things like playing in the moment, breathing in the grass, standing in the sun. Maybe that's how they got so close so quick in 1946.

I watched as they got on the bus after the game. "Jeez, Kid, what were you thinkin'?" Bob James said, laughing, pushing Vic Picetti into his seat. "We won, didn't we?" the 18-year-old said, knowing how to play the game, not knowing yet how to fail at it. "We did, we did," they all said, loving the win and, through it, each other.

There was a flash, and I felt it cross Bob's mind that his brother should be here with them. Bill and Bob, digging out frogs in the creek. We're doing that here, Bob would have thought had he thought about things that way. Still, I could tell that he knew it without thinking it as his mind flashed to years ago, of he and Bill in a muddy creek on a camping trip, catching frogs. These men were becoming his brothers, like his brother was. With everyone ankle deep in mud, out catching frogs.

Close in that moment. Close in the next. Knowing the goodness of the win. Feeling more moments coming to them in the future – moments that would bring them even higher, and closer. "We can't be beat now," some of them would have said that night but didn't, for fear of a jinx. But even without words, they knew it. They felt it. They could taste it. There was something in the air that was theirs to own, to hold onto from now until eternity. They believed it to be luck. In fact, it was their destiny.

But it was more than destiny. It was also a soul. I was so glad to see her arrive. She could reach them in a way that I could not, and could know things that even I did not know. And she was here to stay. She would walk amongst them every day, for 40 days, speaking into them, appreciating their courage, praising their efforts, reminding them of their hearts. As it was with me, they could not see her with their eyes. But they were masters of the moment, and in that moment, at the end of that night, after snatching victory from the jaws of Victoria, they could feel something there that they thought would never leave. And they were right.

Gus Hallbourg brought over the drinks from the bartender. "What a game!" he said, as he grinned at his wife Roberta – Berta for short. It *had* been quite a game, for him. Here they were, all the way out from their Rhode Island home, newlyweds, taking the risk that he could pitch – really pitch. Tonight was one of those nights when it felt like it was worth it. Taking the chance on baseball was worth it, tonight.

"There's Levi," someone said, and Gus waved him over. "Got a drink for you, Levi," Gus said, as they made room at the table for their new friend. The backslapping and greetings had just begun when the bar manager came up. He looked embarrassed. "Levi ..." he began.

Levi smiled. "Evenin'," he said and turned to the others. "We went to college together," he said, gesturing to the bar manager and starting to introduce him around.

The manager held up his hand to stop him. "Now I feel even worse," he said. "I can't help it, Levi. You know I wouldn't do it, if it were up to me."

Levi's smile faded. He turned to the others. "I'll just be leavin'," he said.

"What?" they all said, looking confused.

"He's an Indian," blurted out the bar manager. "There's a law."

"*What*?" Gus said, pointedly now.

"He can't serve me liquor," Levi explained. "There's a law." He patted the manager on the back, and turned towards the door.

Gus stood up. "Now, see here," he began, but Levi stopped him. "There's nothing he can do," Levi said. The bar manager looked miserable. "It's not up to me, Levi," he said.

"Well then, we're leaving too," Gus said, getting up with Berta and leaving the drinks where they sat. Levi demurred, encouraging them to stay. "No, Levi," Gus said as he put on his jacket – a beautiful leather jacket that his mother had given him before he had left for Spokane. "You're our friend. Of course we're going to leave."

Later, Levi wouldn't let anyone speak badly of the bar manager. "He had to do it," Levi said.

I stood with them as they stood outside the house, looking at it. "What do you think, Mel?" Mimi asked, her hand on her growing belly. Her husband grabbed her hand, still looking at the house. "The basement room's big," he said again.

She knew how much it mattered to him to have that big space for the players so they would have a place to relax between games. "The team needs it," he had told her often enough. Especially now he said it, after what happened with Levi the other night. It needed fixing up, this house, but it was big and they maybe could afford it, with the help of GI Bill money. They could fix it up later, if they just could buy it first.

It had taken them by surprise, when the team decided to appoint him manager. But it was perfect. It was a gift from God, really, that he had become manager, even if it left Wright without a job. "They should hire you," she had said. Then it had happened.

And now they might buy this house, big enough for Mel to support the team, if they wanted. It would give them a space, if they needed. "So how did Helen hear of it?" Mel asked. Mimi spoke again of the coincidence of seeing her childhood friend at the store, telling her they couldn't find a house to buy, of Helen knowing of this house being available. Mel squeezed Mimi's hand. She took it and placed it on her belly.

The spirit-soul was there with me as we watched the two of them. At first she and I had wondered if Mel and Mimi would feel her nudgings and find the house at all. Then we had wondered if they would like it – really like it – when they had a chance to see it.

Now that we both had seen their faces, the spirit-soul whisked away. She had been right. It was just what they were looking for.

"Mel," Dwight said. "We got you better than one veteran – we got you two!" Dwight grinned.

"They're *both* coming?" Mel said.

"I think," Dwight said. "Geraghty for sure. Looks like Hartje too. So that's what you'll have. Both of them."

Ben Geraghty and Chris Hartje – both in their 30s, both with the game just a little behind them, both holding on to what they loved.... Both had played for the Brooklyn Dodgers – although Hartje had played just nine games before the war took over. Geraghty had played for Boston as well.

"Good news," Mel said. I felt him wonder if he could hold onto his job.

Ben Geraghty eyed the field and the players on it. He eyed them each up and down. Outfielders seemed loose. Basemen seemed so too. He watched the Mexican kid play at second – the kid he wanted to replace. He seemed stronger than Ben, whose knees kept him slow. Then Ben saw the kid miss a step. He was just half a second off on that throw. I could feel Ben be glad to see a chink in the armor of his competition.

Ben looked around for Mel Cole – his other competition. Mel stood in the batting cage, watching the players, directing field traffic. Quiet guy. Young. Inexperienced. But alert, and aware. Ben was going to have to earn this job if he wanted it.

Ben had been up front about his desire to manage, and he knew that Sam and Dwight had been told about his goals. But both of those men had made casual comments that made Ben question whether they would make him manager. You'll like Mel – he's doing a fine job, they had told Ben. Mel had shown that he knew numbers and the game. I could see Ben wondering, though, if Mel knew how to win. If not, Ben did. He was here to take over second, if his health kept up. He hoped to become manager too.

Mel looked over and saw his new player standing on the edge of the field. He could recognize Ben's thin frame, even from that distance. "Ben," Mel yelled, waving him over just as practice was about to start. "Let me introduce you around."

Headline: June 1, 1946: "PATERSON'S BAT WINS FOR INDIANS" Subheadline: "Three-Run Triple In Ninth Spells Victoria's Doom"

Another win, this time on the back of Bob Paterson, that young center fielder whose job it was to replace the pre-war play of Dwight Aden (the best center fielder that ever was).

It wasn't the first time Bob had stepped out from under Dwight's shadow. On opening night he had gotten top billing, too. "Paterson Provides Indians' Power," the caption had read. But tonight he won the headline – and after three strikeouts, too. What mattered was his last at-bat. That's when he tripled to end the game.

They had had a chance to win it in the eighth. The Chief, the Kid and Bob "Jesse" James had loaded up the bases with two away, but then the next batter had struck out, and all that base-loading was all for naught. But then they won it anyway, in the ninth. And when the game was over, no one seemed to mind the delay. Besides, "Three-Run Triple In Ninth" made for a dramatic headline in the next day's newspaper.

"Can't wait to see you," Vic wrote, as he finished his letter. "Much love...."

He sighed as he put down his pen. He missed Betty. He missed his family. And no one in Spokane knew. Bob Paterson knew a little. He had heard that Vic's father had died the year before – growing up in the same neighborhood as they had, in San Francisco, he would have heard. But even with Bob, Vic had shrugged it off. Instead, each day he wrote to Betty and told her he missed them all, how he hoped his sister Beverly and his little brother Bobby were doing all right without him there, how much it mattered that Betty was there to help his mother (who had such a quiet, strong way of taking care of them all, even as she privately grieved the loss of her husband).... And each day Betty wrote back, telling Vic how much she missed him, how well everyone was doing (even if they weren't), how she looked forward to their wedding in September, how excited they all were to come to Spokane soon, and stay in the cabin he had found for them.... He could relax a little, knowing that Betty was there with his family.

It didn't help in any way that they all had planned on him being in San Francisco that summer. It wasn't until the eve of the season that Casey Stengel had sent him north, making way for a veteran player from before, promising to trade him to Detroit. It was frustrating not to be playing with the Oaks, or in Detroit yet. But then to be gone from the family, too. He and Betty would be all right. Even Beverly – at 15, she had her own friends and places she could go. But Bobby. He was still a baby, only four. If Vic were home, he could fill the void, like he and Betty had been doing, by taking Bobby everywhere with them.

Now, though. There was nothing he could do. Not here. Not from Spokane. Not until the family arrived in July. And there was nothing he could do to explain it to anyone on the team. The team understood his frustration with being sent down to a minor league team. But nobody knew the rest. He didn't even tell anyone on the team that his family would be coming to town and staying in the cabin because, if he did, he would have to explain the details of why. And it was just too much to explain. It was better to keep that all to himself.

So it was with Betty that he shared his feelings. It was with the men that he shared the game. At least, in Spokane, he was playing ball every day. He did love playing ball.

Headline: June 6, 1946: "INDIANS' RALLY BEATS TACOMA"
Subheadline: "Seven Runs In 9th Save Victory For Spokane"

And there it was again – a ninth inning rally. It was something the Indians did often in the spring of 1946 – hand the winning team their defeat in the waning moments of the ninth.

This time they were at home. It was Tacoma 10, Spokane 4 going into that last half inning. The Tribe needed six to tie, seven to win. It was an impossible task....

....."Don't be thinkin' so loud," Bob Kinnaman growled at George Risk as the shortstop stepped into the batter's box to warm up just before the ninth began. Risk rolled his eyes and pointed the bat at Kinnaman like he would shoot him just as easily as forget about him. Bob laughed, as though he knew that George had looked too focused, and that talking to him was a way to jolt George out of his thoughts, get the young shortstop loose, keep him from thinking of anything – threatening rain, six runs down, the need to win, to make the hit. He knew that, for as smart as George was, he was as superstitious as any one of them – that he held in his wallet three two-dollar bills with the corners torn off, just for luck. Bob Paterson joined in Kinnaman's jokes. "See if you can make all three outs at one bat, so we can all go home – ya got the three bills for it," the next-at-bat center fielder said, chuckling, his way of letting Risk know that there was only so much damage the lead-off hitter could do. Even though they all knew otherwise. Even though they all knew it mattered how George Risk hit. George laughed, relaxing a little. "Batter up!" came the umpire's call....

.... but then the impossible turned possible as George Risk started off with a double, Bob Paterson hit to short, Freddie Martinez hit to score Risk, young Vic Picetti got on base by hitting a ball just a little too hard to handle, Bob James hit "for two" and scored the Kid, Mel Cole stepped in for George Lyden and scored James ... and so on. Bob Kinnaman didn't pitch that night so he didn't bat. Chris Hartje didn't join the team for nine more days, so he's not mentioned.

The Tribe almost didn't make it to the ninth that day at all, according to the article. "Rain threatened to end the game in the seventh inning, but stopped after the dust settled and the game was not marred by wet grounds," the article said. It seemed that even the gods were on their side, holding back the rain long enough to let the Tribe win.

"Good game," 22-year-old relief pitcher George Lyden said to his mates as the rally won it for him. I knew he wondered if he would ever get to start a game, or if he was just destined for relief. He had played for the Indians a little before the war. He had been young then, though. Never got the chances that Kinnaman had back then, when Bob had had a terrific season, pitching the win for 22 games. Still, George kept hoping.

Bob Kinnaman came up from behind and pushed him in the back. "Nice work," the pre-war standout told Lyden, letting him know that he was noticed.

"What a game," Jack Lohrke said to Bob James on their way home that night. "And good *stopping* at second," he said, laughing, a comment on how his roommate's enthusiastic running nearly carried him beyond his double in that last inning and would have caused an out they could ill afford – not if they were going to win. "Too bad your brother wasn't here to see it."

Bob nodded, laughing about his comical stop at second, seeming sad about his brother. Then he said, "You know, Jack? It wasn't me."

"It wasn't *you*?"

"Well, yeah it was *me* – just ... if it had been up to me, I'd of kept running. I just forget to stop. But this time – something held me up. Got in my way. Like glue on the base. Up to me, I'd of kept on. And lost the game."

Jack nodded. "I saw you almost overrun the base," he said. "Figured you just caught yourself up."

"Yep," Bob answered, "just that I wasn't the one to do it. I got a little extra help out there."

They looked at each other. It had been like that for days – one good luck moment after the other. "We can't lose, can we?" Bob said to his mate, almost in a whisper. There – it had been said. "We're just might win the pennant," he said.

Jack nodded. "One more win, we take the lead," he said. "Seems like someone's on our side."

They kept walking, in silence now, as they wondered at their extraordinary luck. I smiled as I watched them. The spirit-soul did too, and let me know she was glad to have more than nudged Bob during the game to keep him from running past second.

Headline: June 6, 1946: "INDIANS CLIMB TO LEAGUE LEAD"
Subheadline: "Beat Tacoma Here, But Victoria Helps"

They had done it! They had taken over the lead! The fourth, not the ninth, had been their big inning this night. The Chief "cleaned house," the newspaper said. The "pond" was "full of ducks," the writer expounded – bases loaded, he meant. Then Levi McCormack hit a "screaming double," energy moved, and runs were scored. And then, hope against hope, Victoria beat Salem, the first-place team – the team that had destroyed the Tribe in their first road trip, back in early May, back before they believed this pennant might be theirs to win. It sure helped, the way Gus Hallbourg pitched that night, leaving the team with that continuing need to find a place to go for the post-game celebration.

Suddenly, and just a month later, it turned out that it *was* their pennant to win.

The Indians. The Spokane Nine. There they were. In first place.

They crashed for a few games after that. Too much excitement, maybe, to hold on to first place for longer than a night. A few losses. But not too many. And a few days later, they climbed back up – to second place.

I joined Betty Lyden as she brought their two boys with her to the field, like she always did. "Look, there's Daddy," she said, pointing out George to the boys. They waved. The young boys' faces were bright and red, from the sun and from the washcloth Betty had used to clean them up. They were good boys. Their father would sit on the bench tonight. Let them watch him sit, was what Betty thought. She knew he loved what he did, playing or sitting, though he never really talked about it. The only way for his boys to get a sense of his love for the game was to watch him as he stood in the midst of it. Besides, who knew? Maybe he would end up pitching in the last inning, if the pitcher got in trouble. The brothers watched as their daddy talked to his mates. It's good for them to see, I could hear Betty think, as she had them wave at him one more time, when he happened to look up to where they were.

Betty looked around the field as everyone got ready for the opening pitch. I saw her see two older boys, off in the distance. They looked like her two boys would look a few years from now. They were throwing the ball back and forth. Now high in the air, like a fly ball. Laughing loud at the miss. We wondered if they were brothers.

We saw Bob James yell something from the outfield at the two boys. We couldn't hear what he was saying, but the boys heard and lined up for a pop-up throw from the big right fielder. Then Bob Paterson threw one up. Betty smiled, and her smile reminded me of how good the two Bobs were to her own two boys. They'll make great fathers someday, I think she thought. I know *I* did.

I remembered another sunny day out in the ballpark, not too long ago, when George's brother Jim had brought his son Gary to watch a game. Gary had spilled over with excitement at the idea of seeing Uncle George play baseball. But it had been one of those nights when George not only didn't get to play, he didn't even get to suit up. Still it was a night to remember, as George came and found them later, thanking them for coming to watch. "You should join," he had said to Gary's dad again. Jim shook his head no. "I've played with 'em here, and in the war, Jim," George pressed on. "You're better than most, I can tell you that. You could try out today, and sign up tomorrow," he urged. "Let me ask Mel – you'll see."

Jim just smiled and waved him off. "We only need one Babe Ruth Lyden," he said, and both brothers laughed. It was a reference to an old family story – that the priest kept insisting, after George was born, that their mother come up with a name for the new baby for the records. Finally she had asked the priest, "What's Babe Ruth's real name?" George Herman Ruth, the priest had said. "Then I'll name him George," Mrs. Lyden had said.

• • •

Sometimes what Mel did worked. Sometimes it didn't. Each time it worked, he looked worried about the next time. Each time it didn't work, he would try to get better.

Somehow, though, in the midst of it all, Dwight and Sam had decided it was fine to have him as the manager. They had even stopped looking for a replacement. That second baseman they got – Ben Geraghty, older than Mel, more experienced – they still had brought him on, but as a player, not manager. He would take over from Mel. Help him, it seemed, but not replace him.

Still, Mel could take no chances. His wife said so, too. So he worked hard, kept focused. I'm here to set the goals, he would say aloud to himself, when he thought no one was listening. Otherwise, he would say it in his head. Either way, he knew it was his job.

Headline: June 8, 1946: "POWERS TOSSES INDIAN VICTORY"
Subheadline: "Wild Fifth Frame Gives Tilt To Spokane"

Winning again. This time, a home game, won in the fifth. Or won enough in the fifth to count on the outcome. Not that anyone gave up. Just let loose a little. There was a freedom in playing a game already won.

It was a "riotous" game, the newspaper explained. The ump had to break up a fight between catcher and batter at the top of the sixth. And Ben Geraghty, the new arrival, stepped in at second with a "hot double play" in the eighth and a "single, double and a triple in four times at the plate."

"I sure needed that stretch from the Kid at first base for that play to work," the spirit-soul and I heard Ben say to himself ruefully, though he did seem glad for the strong beginning. He needed to be strong if he was going to make a name for himself here.

We knew that Ben didn't understand yet what it meant to play for this team. He didn't quite understand that there was something magical about this group of men. Who could blame him? Nothing had happened yet. Nothing but the collection of souls, that is.

Instead, Ben – and the others, too, it's true – just saw what was right in front of them. That they were in second place again. Primed – again – to take over first.

Onto the field, waiting for yet another practice to start. Nice day. No clouds. No afternoon rainstorm today. Sun instead. In the heat. Like San Diego, down south.

"Hey, Martinez – out here!" yelled one of the Bobs from left field, signaling for a ball. Freddie leaned down, picked one up, and threw it into left. He shielded his eyes. He saw it caught. He sat down on the bench to wait for practice to start.

Freddie Martinez was a quiet man. Partly it was his nature. Partly it was his hesitant English. Partly it was because there were plenty of others doing the talking. His roommates Bob and Jack, for instance. He saw them as good men. They were from the Southwest, like he was. They took him places; spoke Spanish to him. Broken Spanish, but they tried. He liked them all, but Bob and Jack he liked the best.

Freddie was like Levi – quieter than Levi, but still helping the rest with his kind spirit. Just being there helped. Unlike Levi, though, Freddie didn't know that he helped in that way. He didn't know it, and they didn't know it. Still, it was the way it was. And there was nothing better than a day like today. It was almost perfect, that hot June day.

He could have been worried. The new player, Ben Geraghty, looked like he was taking over second. And Freddie did seem a little worried by that. But Mel had told him he would just play him more in the outfield, so long as Sam and Dwight OK'd it. They needed him in the game, Mel assured him. They needed his offense, for one. Which was true – the way Freddie was batting, they would have to think twice before leaving him on the bench. Besides, everyone knew about the baby coming and that it could help Freddie if he got a chance to get noticed. And his bat was something to notice. So Freddie would become an outfielder, is all. Or maybe someone from the infield would be called up (which meant to the Pacific Coast League, the closest the West had to the major league). Maybe they would call up Jack. Freddie looked out towards third, where his roommate was. Jack's defense was solid, he was batting over 360, and everyone figured that he was on San Diego's short list of all their minor league players to call up.

Freddie sighed as he watched his friend, and I knew he hated to think of Jack leaving. But it would be good for Jack. And good for Freddie, too. For his game, that is, since it would get him back into the infield. Whatever happened, Freddie was just glad to be in Spokane, playing ball. He was worried a little, but mostly he was glad.

And now it was time to play.

He got up from the bench, walked into the sun, took off his cap, and stood with his face to the sky, eyes closed, soaking the moment into his skin. Then he put on his cap, shoved it down low on his brow, and trotted out to left field to join his mates.

Headline: June 12, 1946: "TACOMA TAKES SPOKANE NINE"
Subheadline: "Reach Bob Kinnaman For 13 Safeties"

Not good baseball, that night. The writer valiantly tried to speak of valiant efforts, but to no real avail. Ultimate score, 5 to 3. The game wasn't that close, since two of Spokane's runs came in the ninth. "Again in the Indians' half of the last, an attempt was made to pull the club out of the red and two Spokane scores crossed the rubber," said the article. "The rally attempt was too late, however, and the side was retired before the threat could become decisive." Too little, too late. Cut off at the knees, so to speak.

Sometimes a rally in the ninth makes a difference. Sometimes not. Even still, they were the "Spokane Nine," according to the headline. They actually had played ten that day, but just barely (with just one at-bat from a pinch hitter). So seeing "Spokane Nine" in the headline – it had a nice ring to it. Even in defeat we're a team, it said. It takes nine of us, you know.

"Could be worse," Kinnaman had said as they all filed off the field. "We could be on some shore, waiting for a bomb to drop." He said it to make everyone feel better, including himself, as he thought through his pitches – mostly bad ones tonight.

They all nodded. Bob was right. There was that. It was one of the starkest things about the season – how good they felt to be out of the war. Vic Picetti, their young first baseman, didn't know about that because he hadn't been in the war. Some of the others, too, understood less than the rest since their posts had been local, not overseas. But even they understood that, even when they lost, they won. They already had won. They were home.

I could feel Bob thinking through his pitches. He was wondering if he was just having some off nights or if his arm was done, or if he would ever get a chance to repeat the season of 1941.

"*Where?*" Grace had asked him.

"Spokane," Chris Hartje had answered. "Up in Washington. Near Idaho." They had looked it up on a map, then, just to be sure.

Grace knew it was her husband's dream to play ball again. "Or manage," he would say, but she knew it was to play. It was all he had ever known. She didn't know what he would do if he weren't playing ball somewhere. Besides, he had had his moment in the sun, back before the war, had tasted the Big Leagues with the Brooklyn Dodgers – nine games was all, but it was something – and now he wanted to get back to it, now that the war was over.

Though it was his dream, too, not to have to play so far away from home. He had never liked playing for teams outside the San Francisco Bay area. Once he had even come back home in the middle of a season because he had gotten egged on by his buddies to do it – just do it! they had said. And he had. And had gotten in trouble for it. His impulsiveness had earned him a reputation as being un-reliable. Which really wasn't fair, Grace thought, as she grumbled again at how his friends had talked him into taking the trip home.

But even with the distance, and even with her being seven months pregnant, she could feel him get excited at the thought of signing on with a team somewhere. He had almost gotten on with Casey Stengel's Oaks, but then there had been a heated exchange of words and – well, at least it looked like he would get a chance in Spokane.

"I wish you could come, hon," he said. She nodded. But they already had checked with the doctor. She couldn't travel, this far along in the pregnancy. They had tried so hard to get pregnant dur-ing their eight years of marriage. They couldn't risk her traveling now. She would stay instead with her parents.

"One good thing," she said to him again, reminding him of what he had told her. "You do know someone already." Chris nodded. He and Dutch Anderson, Spokane's trainer, knew each other from way back. Chris smiled. It would be great to see Dutch.

Headline: June 17, 1946: "SPOKANE DROPS PAIR TO TIGERS"
Subheadline: "Indians' Losing Streak Extended To Six Straight"

Being that close to first place was still more than they could han-dle, it seemed. Now all they seemed able to do was slide backwards. With Mel Cole, Vic Picetti, and Freddie Martinez all kicked out of the game for fighting with the umpire. The Tribe had taken early lead, but had lost it. All for naught, that night. But still they had a shot. Salem, the team that had taken them in that first road trip, the team now in first place, was coming to Spokane for a seven-game series. If the Indians won the series, maybe they could take the pennant.

• • •

Headline: June 18, 1946: "SPOKANE FACES UPWARD CLIMB"

It was a day off for the Tribe, but not the newspaper – time to insert opinion:

> The Spokane Indians, after a heartbreaking session at Salem recently returned to Ferris field the following week near the bottom of the heap, and clambered up again, to rest momentarily at the top. Tonight, at the home ball park, the Indians will have to do it again. Returning from losing four games in a row to the Tacoma Tigers, while games either team might have won were rained out, the fifth-place Spokane nine is eyeing the comeback route against the Salem Senators, not too firmly ensconced on the top of the standings.

The article helped to build anticipation for the upcoming series. Who would win the best-of-seven series?

The paper gave an update, too, on the league's decision to uphold a fine imposed on Manager Mel Cole the night before. The newspaper recalled how the fine, imposed during that home game, had "caused many spectators to boil over with indignation," and stated again about what a bad call it had been.

The update reminded fans of that moment when their young leader had been so riled by a bad call from the umpire in the previous night's game that he had lost his temper and had gotten tossed. (Yer out! the ump had said as he threw Cole out). It cannot be helped, the pride that comes when your manager's passion overtakes him like that – especially when that man is an otherwise decent, likable but mostly quiet fellow who leads by example, not drama. It would have been better if Mel had been able to stay on the field, so he could lead in person. But we all could not help but love him for getting himself thrown out when his passion overtook his usual poker-face demeanor. Baseball cannot get much better than knowing that your leader knows how to stand up and be counted.

A whole group of them had made it to the rec room in the Coles' new basement that first night. There was Risk and Paterson, and their wives upstairs, talking with Mel's wife; Bob, Jack and Freddie (the three roommates, almost always together, with Freddie's wife in San Diego, waiting for the birth of their baby); and the Kid – they had dragged him along with them, even though he had said he didn't want to go.

Most everyone had other places to be. They had asked the new man, Ben Geraghty, and he said he might come. They knew he wouldn't, though. The way he said yes, they knew he meant no. "You're always welcomed," Mel had said.

Levi and Gus weren't there, either. They had gone to Idaho at the last minute, having a rare day off. There was always the next time, Mel had thought, smiling, as he had gazed around the home that he and Mimi finally had been able to secure.

The women were in the kitchen, talking about the baby coming – what did Mimi want, a boy or a girl? A boy, she said, just like his dad. We can have a girl later, she mused, but I'd like to start with a boy – like Betty and George, she said, and we all thought of the Lydens' two young sons. "Boy or girl, though, this child had better like to play ball, or Mel's going to try to get *me* out there in the yard to play catch," she added, laughing, and started talking then about their plans for the yard, once the season had ended and Mel had more time.

A while later she turned to Marjorie Risk. "What about you two? Any talk of a baby on the way?" Marjie blushed. It *was* something they talked about, she said. Then they both turned to their third comrade, Dorothy Paterson. "Don't look at me!" she said, laughing, also a little embarrassed.

Mimi showed them around the new home, then. There wasn't much to see yet, but she could tell them what they planned. "Yes," she said, in answer to their questions. "We do plan to make Spokane our permanent home."

There was rustling and rumblings of conversations beneath them. Every so often, a loud shout came, followed by laughter. Less often, one man or another would appear at the basement door. Got any more hot dogs? or beer? he would say as he stood with his hand of cards.

Once, Bob Paterson came up the stairs. "Hon," he said, "we got the paper today, didn't we? With the article about yesterday's game?" His wife nodded. "I cut it out," she said, without adding, like I always do.

"We got it!" Bob yelled into the basement as he bounded back down the stairs.

• • •

Mel sat down on the bench next to his talented first baseman, his youngest player. "Vic Is Sick," the headline had read, and had gone on to say that Vic was batting badly. Everyone knew something was up for the Kid.

Only seven years separated the two men. But it seemed like decades to the men who watched them from around the field. Vic was just a baby, they thought; Mel, just back from the war, new homeowner, first-year manager, baby on the way, was a man.

"I hear you got a letter from your ma," Mel said after a while.

"Yeah," Vic said quietly, and scuffed at the ground. Mel saw him shove the sports section of the newspaper off to the side.

"What do reporters know," Mel said. "We're lucky you're here, Vic. You've got the hustle, and the stretch. And the bat's there. You'll work it out."

"I came early to hit some extra balls," Vic said.

"Good idea," Mel said, nodding. He reached over and picked up a bat. "Ben is good at coaching the bat," Mel said, handing Vic the bat and gesturing to Ben Geraghty, the newcomer. "He might have some words for you." Mel watched Vic walk off with the bat towards Ben. Then he went off in the opposite direction to where Sam was standing.

"What do you think?" the owner said to his young manager.

"Sam," Mel said, "I think the boy just misses his mother."

Sam laughed. Vic was such a kid to him. Came from a big Italian family. Babied by his mother, is what Sam imagined – could imagine, knowing nothing more, knowing only what he believed about Italian families and their mothers. "He'll have to get over that," Sam said.

"Sure, he feels bad, too – kicked out by Oakland at the last minute like that, and still waiting to hear." Mel paused. "You know, he'd be eating supper with his family in San Francisco every night, if Oakland had kept him on."

Sam nodded. "Their loss, our gain," was all he said.

The spirit-soul and I stood with them, listening in as they talked. We knew that not even Mel could understand, not fully. All he knew was what Bob Paterson had said – that Vic's father had died the year before. He didn't really know how much of a void there was in the Picetti home without Vic there. Mel, like Sam, imagined that the Kid was just a boy, not a boy who had become a man overnight to hold his family together.

Still, Mel had a way of understanding things he did not know. So the spirit-soul whispered towards Mel – thought-words more than sound, speaking to him like intuition does. And suddenly Mel said, "I know what we can do."

"What's that?" Sam said, curious.

"Vic misses his family, right?" Mel said, using logic to explain his thought. "And his swing's off because of it. What if we sent him home? Say, for an early birthday present."

"When's his birthday?" Sam asked.

"I don't know," Mel answered. "Make it a Christmas present then. He goes home to San Francisco, sees that family of his, and then comes back full of it, like normal."

Sam nodded. He could see that it was a good idea. "Do it," he said. "Right after the Bremerton series. We'll send him home from Seattle."

"Hey, Vic – boy, are you in trouble with me," Bob James said as he walked past Vic at first on his way to right field.

Vic gave him a confused look. "Why?"

"I had to pay a dollar because of you," Bob said, grinning at the thought the money he had chipped in for Vic's trip home.

"A dollar?" Vic said, still confused.

"A dollar well spent, as far as I can tell," Bob said, then realized that Vic really didn't know what he was talking about. "Hasn't anyone told you yet?"

"Told me what?" Vic asked.

"Can't say. But it's good. You'll be glad about it," Bob said, winking.

Headline: June 19, 1946: "TRIBE CLUBS SALEM, 10 TO 9"

They edged out the win, that first night of the Salem series. They didn't do it in the ninth, though. No, this time they found themselves hanging on for the win in the ninth, as Salem scored four of their nine runs in the top of that last inning. The Tribe got the win nonetheless. "With a tremendous uprising in the fifth inning which netted seven runs, the Indians pounced all over the alleged top team of the Western International League." It gave them just enough to win without even having to go down to the wire.

• • •

Chris Hartje, bat in hand, stepped into the dugout. Levi came up to shake his hand. Ben, no longer the newest on the team with Chris' arrival, laughed. "Levi here's the welcoming committee," he said, as Gus extended his hand as well.

"Glad to meet ya," Chris said, shaking hands with Levi and Gus and nodding at the rest. They all nodded back. Ben walked up and grabbed Chris' mitt. "Pretty well worn," he said, sounding impressed.

"I hear we missed each other up in Brooklyn," Chris said, a comment on the late '30s, when Ben had played for the Dodgers a couple years before Chris.

"That's true," Ben responded. "When did you play?"

"1939. Just at the end. Nine games, is all."

"What'd you bat?" Ben asked.

"Three thirteen," Chris said.

Ben whistled. Others murmured approval. Chris grinned and looked around. "Dutch anywhere?" he asked.

And now all was set. All that had been left was for Chris to arrive.

Headline: June 20, 1946: "SPOKANE WINS FROM SALEM"
Subheadline: "Milt Cadinha Pitches Indian Victory, 6 To 2"

Another game that was never in doubt (as it was in those days, when Milt Cadinha took the mound). But it wasn't just the pitcher's play. There was a new catcher in town – Chris Hartje, former Brooklyn Dodgers man from before the war. Everything had happened before the war. He had arrived just a few days before to play that catcher spot. And he had done well. "Hartje Wins Fans," the subheading read. He was playing for the "first time this season," the newspaper reported, "and before the game was half over he had the crowd with him. His hustle was something the Indians can certainly use and his job in handling Cadinha left nothing to be desired. At the plate he proved to be a tough man to handle, getting on base every time up." And while none of the runners "tested out his arm" by attempting to steal second, the newspaper was sure that Hartje would have been able to make the throw. A man "with all the other qualities" was sure to show a "rifle arm," if someone ever dared to test it.

It was a great way for Chris to start. His energy was high, his hopes higher. I knew that he hoped Spokane would be the answer he was looking for – his way back into the game, he thought as he had played, as he started to learn the men who would become his mates. Good men, he thought, as he went to find Dutch to celebrate.

The only part that made Chris sad was that Grace wasn't there. But she just couldn't make it. The doctor said it was too risky for the baby. Still, Chris was excited when they talked. "Two other wives are pregnant, hon," he told her when he called home to let her know he had arrived. "What are the chances of that? One is the manager's wife Mimi – Mel Cole's his name – he's young," Chris told her. "Only 25," but a good man with a baby on the way just like them. Who's the other with a baby on the way? Grace had asked. So he had told her about Freddie and Freddie's roommates Jack and Bob.

Levi McCormack also had a great game that night. "Chief Gets Triple," the subheading read. Spokane loved this man, this great Indian warrior whose father, they believed, had been a Nez Perce Chief. So they called him Chief and loved him even more as he ran out the triple and then saw Freddie Martinez sacrifice him home.

Levi sat down in the clubhouse near Ben and started to change.

"Levi," Ben said, stretching out his legs to keep them from tightening up. "Good game. Kept waitin' to try out the new guy's throw to second. 'Steal the base, steal the base,' I kept sayin'. Did you see me out there? I even walked over to that runner on first. Told him, 'steal the base.' He looked at me like I was a ghost, was the way he looked." Ben grinned, remembering the look. Levi grinned back.

"Go out for a drink?" Ben asked. Levi shook his head no. "One of these times, you'll come with me," Ben warned as he gathered up his belongings.

Levi shrugged. "One of these times, you'll come with the rest of us to play cards," he responded.

His time had come. George Lyden was ready to start.

"That's what Mel said," Bob Kinnaman told the young pitcher. "They think you're ready to start, George," Kinnaman said. I could tell he was glad to be the one who delivered the news to this local farm boy of few words. Bob, better than anyone, would know how earnest George was, both before the war and now, and I could tell Bob was glad that George would get a chance to start. "Either tonight or the first game of the double-header," Bob said.

George got a concerned look on his face. Bob almost missed it, but something (someone, not me, but the spirit-soul) gave him a nagging sense that he had to look closely at George – and then he saw that George was worried.

"Somethin' on your mind?" Bob asked.

"Just … not enough time to get my family here from Idaho if I'm starting tonight," George said.

He was right. And there was no reason George should have his first chance to start without his family there since they were just down the road.

"I'll talk to Mel," Bob said, nodding. "Just tell your kin to come on Sunday."

George Lyden walked into the house with a loud whooping sound. His boys came running with Betty right behind them, wiping her hands on a kitchen towel, looking worried at all the noise.

"What's wrong?" Betty asked, as the boys jumped up at him.

"Nothing's wrong," George said, as he jostled with one boy and picked up the other. "Nothing's wrong at all," he said again, grinning. "Things could not be better, that's how much nothing is wrong," he said, as he told her about Sunday's start.

Then they lost. Then they won. Then they lost again. By June 23rd, the Indians were up in the seven game series, 3 to 2. They had a double-header that day.

Then they lost. And then they won.

Headline: June 24, 1946: "SPOKANE WINS SALEM SERIES, 4-3"
Subheadline: "Split Double-Header Here Yesterday, 7-9 And 10-9"

So when had they done it? When had they pulled it together to win the last game? To the victor goes the series….

In the ninth, of course. "Three runs in the ninth inning gave the Spokane Indians a hectic 10-to-9 victory over the Salem Senators in the final game of the seven-game series at Ferris field last night."

Another subheading: "Spokane Fights Back:"

> With two out in their half of the eighth the Indians started a rally that netted one run and after the Senators were retired in the ninth Spokane made its final bid a winning one.

The article details the nuances of that ninth inning – who hit what, for how many bases, at what count, with how many batted in as a result. It was a joy of an article to write, to be sure, and a joy for the fans to read in the morning. And what fun it was to see Jack Lohrke's play that night:

> <u>Lohrke Afire</u>: Jack Lohrke, Spokane's sensational third baseman, continued his great play afield and contributed four hits in the evening contest, including a line drive 380 feet over the clock to the left of the scoreboard in left center field. The ball must have just barely missed putting the timepiece out of order.

It was hyperbole, to speak in such a way of knocking out the timepiece – an effort to demonstrate how far the ball had gone, and where....

In the afternoon game – the one they had lost – young pitcher George Lyden had had his first start. He had done well, and his family had come from their Idaho farm. It was just the last couple innings that didn't go well, as his arm got tired. It was okay to lose that game, then – it was really a game lost to the growth of the team.

The article reported that, the day after the double-header, the Indians were getting on the bus to go to Bremerton, near Seattle. They had done well in taking this series. If they won in Bremerton and Salem kept losing, the Tribe could recapture the lead.

It was the next day. They were gathering to the bus. Stepping up into it....

Mel Cole stood by the side of the bus, watching the players load up. Lanky Bob James was first, leaping into the bus, skipping all the steps, with Freddie Martinez and Jack Lohrke, right after him. The three roommates, that was them. It had been Jack's night the night before, after knocking in those winning runs. They'll call you up now, Bob had said, trying hard not to be envious. "They're calling you up right now," he said. "De veras, Freddie?" Bob said, keeping Freddie tied close to them, laughing and losing his envy when something (someone) got him to see the flicker of hope in Jack's eyes.

The spirit-soul had me stand with her next to Mel, at the side of the bus. We watched them load up, one by one. There they were – each and every one. How to keep at least some of them away, was the thought that she sent to me. The boyhood friends, pitchers Milt Cadinha and Joe Faria, were driving on their own with their wives. And Dutch Anderson, the trainer, had been called home to San Francisco at the last minute, a one-day job to keep his union membership at the newspaper, so he wouldn't be on the bus. Chris Hartje had lent him a twenty, to help him find his way home.

But the rest of them loaded up – pitchers, basemen, outfielders.... She sighed, and I sighed with her, as Glen Berg, the young bus driver, worried quietly about the condition of the brakes. Even after having driven the bus for a few blocks, between the bus yard and the ball field, he was worried. But there was nothing he could do about them, even if he got off the bus and peered with a flashlight into their mechanics. That, we knew.

Mel squinted at the men as they loaded up, and as he and Dwight loaded up all the gear. Seeing Dwight reminded Mel of how Mel had kept Kenny, the bat boy, from coming on this trip. Kenny had come to Mel the night before, after the double-header, and had pleaded with Mel to let him come, saying that his parents already had agreed.

"Did Mr. Aden say that you could come?" Mel had asked the boy, who had blushed and stammered, and shook his head no, not yet, that he couldn't find Mr. Aden to ask.

Mel could have relented – could have told him to show up in the morning, since he knew Dwight would be at the bus to send them off. But the spirit-soul had nudged Mel and had given him a sense that he just had to say no. So Mel had squinted, looked tough, and spat on the ground. "Not this time, Kenny. No trip without Mr. Aden's okay. I can't have you just showing up tomorrow morning without the right permission."

"But Mr. Cole," the boy had begun. Mel remembered how he would hear none of it, and had waved the boy off, had been uncharacteristically unsympathetic. "You just can't come," Mel had said, and had watched Kenny walk away with his head hung down, back to where his parents stood. Mel wondered at it now – it would have been so easy to let Kenny show up this morning when Mel had known Dwight was going to be here....

Mel's thoughts were interrupted as Bob Kinnaman came up. "Did you call your folks yet?" Mel asked, knowing Bob's parents lived on the west side of the state.

"All done," Bob said with a grin. "They were thinking about going to the second game anyway, but they said they would be sure to make the drive now, since I called. And they said to say thank you for the tickets." Bob thought of how great it would for his father, who had not been feeling well, to get to go to the game.

Chris Hartje stepped onto the bus next. "How's your knee Chris?" Mel asked him.

"Banged up some, but not too bad," Chris said as he loaded up. He swung his leg a little. "See?" he said, hiding his wince, wanting badly to take the trip, to stay with the team and his momentum.

Mel nodded. "Keep it iced. Long trip'll make it stiff. I should know," he said, grimacing about his own wound. "And have Dutch look at it when he gets to Bremerton."

Chris nodded. "He's looked at it already. Poor Dutch, having to spend so much time on my aches and pains." He laughed and took a seat for the long ride ahead.

Vic loaded up next, with a lighter step than usual. He was thinking about how, after this road trip, his family would be that much closer to coming to Spokane. He had to wait just a week until July. It would be just around the corner from there. And even if he ended up staying in Spokane the rest of the season, at least he was playing every day. He did love the game. He was just feeling a little better about it all, and he didn't even know about the surprise trip home. He sat down near Chris. "What's the problem with your knee?" he asked as he settled in, knowing Chris from Oakland's preseason camp.

Chris grinned at the Kid, even using Vic's nickname here, even though it was just his ninth day as a member of the team, and even fewer since he had gotten to Spokane. "What do you hear from home?" Chris asked, though it was just his way to start talking about the pang of homesickness in his own heart. If it weren't for baseball, he would be home now with Grace, waiting for the baby to arrive. Still it was good to talk to Vic about their home town of San Francisco, finding out where Vic lived exactly, talking about how they both had been in Stengel's preseason camp, how they both had been sent here instead, how they both hoped to get back with the Oaks soon, how Vic might have a chance with Detroit, and so on.

And for Vic, it was almost a miracle to listen to Chris talk about how much he missed being where he wanted to be. Maybe I could say something to Chris, Vic thought, as he imagined sharing a little about how he was missing home too, and why. He didn't share, but he thought about it. So it was nice to hear Chris talk.

The team would have to go through Snoqualmie Pass on their way to the Coast. It was a bad pass even in the best of weather, even with the best of vehicles. On June 24th, on their way to Bremerton, the weather was a problem. Fog. Drizzle. The bus was worse. Bad brakes. You can't wish away fog or rain and, in 1946, you couldn't fix bad brakes. The war had depleted the country of the metal needed to build parts to make mechanical repairs. Everyone knew it. It was all over the newspapers. There was no way to drive to Bremerton and still be sure they would be safe. Best they could do was hope for the best. Or not get on the bus at all.

"Mel Cole. Is Mel Cole still here?" called out the highway patrol officer.

"Right here," Mel said, checking for his wallet as they all got ready to load back up on the bus from supper at the diner in Ellensburg, the town just before the mountains.

"Got a message for you, Mr. Cole," the officer said. "Glad I caught you before you got back on the bus."

"I was just on my way," Mel said.

"I'm supposed to tell you to kick Jack Lohrke off the bus and have him make his way back to Spokane," the officer said, clearly impressed that he would be delivering such a message.

"Something wrong?" Mel asked.

"Nothin' like that," the officer answered, smiling, enjoying the surprise of the moment, handing Mel his scribbled notes. "Jack's got to go back to Spokane to pack his bags. San Diego's called him up."

"Thanks," Mel said, looking at the officer's notes and then hurrying outside. "Hey, Jack!" Mel yelled to his third baseman.

"Yeah?" Jack turned around, one foot on the first step of the bus entrance.

"Get outta here," Mel said, smiling. "You're going to San Diego."

Jack stood stunned. "You're kidding me," he said, finally.

"I'm not," Mel answered, showing him the note. "You're on your way. They must of heard how you tried to knock out the game clock," Mel joked. "Grab your gear. We got to get moving – this bus is slow, it's the best bus they've got, and we're not going to get in until close to midnight, at the rate we're going, especially now that we've got to cross the Pass. So get your gear quick and get to Spokane."

Jack jumped onto the bus, hit Bob James in the shoulder and tapped Freddie on his arm. "I gotta get back to Spokane," he said. "They called me up, just like you said."

"You're lying," Bob said.

"Maybe Mel is lying, but I'm not – that's what he just told me," Jack said, as he grabbed his bag.

"How are you going?" Freddie wanted to know.

"I don't know," Jack said. "Hitchhike, I guess."

"Wait a minute," Bob said. "You can't just go. We'll never see you again."

Jack laughed. "Well, *you* have to go West, and *I* have to head back to Spokane to pack up before leaving for San Diego, so I *can* just go," he said. "But I'll see you again. You'll come there – or I'll come visit you and Bill in Arizona. And Freddie – we're almost neighbors where we live in San Diego, right, Freddie? Besides, they'll probably bring me up for a week, then send me back here – you know how it goes," he said, his normal easy chuckle getting stuck in his throat at the thought of leaving these mates.

"Wait," said Levi, who had stopped his conversation with an-other player so he could hear Jack's news. He reached into his bag, pulled something out, and handed it to Jack. It was one of Levi's red shirts.

"Your shirt," was all Jack said as he took the bundle from Levi.

"You return that shirt in person," Levi said sternly.

"I will," Jack said solemnly. Then they both grinned. "Hey," Jack yelled back into the belly of the bus. He waved his arm above his head and gave out a holler. They all hollered back. Jack flipped the shirt into his bag as he leapt off the bus so his mates could get back to the business of getting on the road to Bremerton. And so it was in that way that they all said goodbye.

As Jack watched the bus lumber towards the West, I felt him flash on another unexpected goodbye he had had. This one had been right after the war. He had been back in the States, but not yet back home, getting ready to fly out on a small plane but getting bumped instead by some higher-ranked officer (not enough room for you too, the pilot had said). "Good luck," those mates had said as they had flown away. He had envied them. They would get home before he did. It's not fair, he had thought at the time, grumbled even, as he sat waiting for the next flight, whenever that would be. Later, he learned that the plane had crashed. All on board had died.

I felt him wonder why he had to think of that now. I could tell it made him cringe, to think of it. I looked at the spirit-soul. It dawned on me that she was the one to get him to remember. I turned back in time to see Jack shake his head as if to shake away the thought, then turn away from the bus and look towards Spokane, scanning the cars for a likely ride to take him back there.

In about that moment, in the early evening hours, George Lyden's brother Jim suddenly felt sick. Something was about to happen. He knew it. He hoped against it. But he knew it just the same.

"I thought the bus was slow gettin' us to *supper*," Bob Kinnaman grumbled as the bus started crawling up the mountainside amid the fog and drizzle. Bob looked out the window. "You should try the fishin' 'round here," he told Gus, who was sitting in front of him. It started the two pitchers talking. Bass, salmon, fresh water fishing – their talk kept them entertained as the bus climbed up the narrow two-lane highway, winding around the bends.

As they reached the summit and began their descent, Gus looked out the window to the steep drop below on the right. "This'd be a helluva place to go over," he said to Bob.

Just then, a black car came uphill from the opposite direction and edged across the center line, making its way towards the left front corner of the bus.

PART 3

Three Days

Some of the priests came to Joan's prison cell to render the verdict. She sat quietly as one of the priests told her that she would be put to death. When? she asked. Now, he said. This morning. She nodded, as though she were ready – as though she knew there was no choice. By what method? she asked. By fire, he said.

"Oh, I knew it!" she said, and began to cry. "Is there no other way?" she asked him, looking at him with fear in her eyes and soul. I am sorry Jehanne, he said, and nearly began to cry himself, but no. No. This is the only way. "Please," she did say, once more. And her eyes, too – they begged for mercy, looking from face to face, seeking any answer but the answer that she had. But no one would look at her, or try to help her. Her she was, the one who had tried to help every soldier left to die on the battlefield, had not one person came her rescue when she was the one seeking mercy. At least the priests gave her the blessed Sacrament first. Perhaps Bishop Cauchon feared his own demise before God if he kept the Sacrament from her in her last moments.

As they led her to the stake, she did ask in a quiet voice for a cross to hold. There was no cross there, but a British soldier, touched by her tears, took two pieces of wood and tied them with leather into the shape of a cross. Thank you, she said humbly, took the cross, and kissed its form. Then she climbed up the steps to the face of the stake, one step at a time, weeping with each step that she took (quietly, quietly wept). Once at the stake, the executioner had to lift her up onto the top of the woodpile because she was so small and the wood was piled so high. He then wound chains around her, to tie her firmly to the stake. She stood there alone, at the top of the woodpile, as he got ready to set it on fire.

Those who were there say that a young priest, Friar Isambard, came through the crowd and gave her a cross that he had blessed with holy water, to replace the makeshift one. They say that she accepted his offer to hold the cross for her to see, but then begged him to leave the platform for his own safety, just before the fire started. "Hold it in front of me there," she said, looking to the ground right in front, and he complied.

They say, too, that, just as the fire was lit, Bishop Cauchon came to her one last time – he who put her on trial and caused the loss of her life, and light – to shout at her, "Repent! Repent! Lest you burn not just here but in hell too!" And they say that her last sentence was spoken to him: "I die through you," she said, gazing straight ahead, with a calmness in her voice.

As the flames arose and overtook her form, they say they could hear her praying to the God she claimed to love, and to whom she delivered her soul. They could, at times, see her upturned face in amongst the flames and smoke. Some say they heard her pray for the salvation of those who stood before her, choosing to watch her die. And then, they say, they heard no more. Just the crackling of the flames of a wild bonfire.

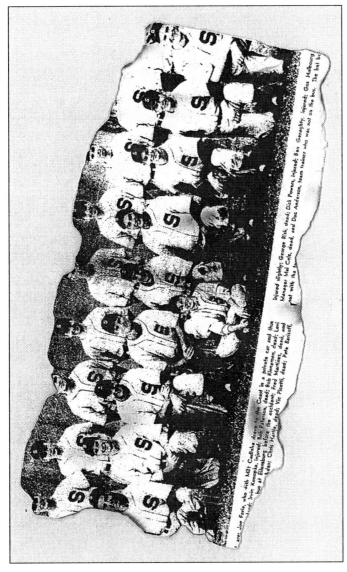

Photograph of the Spokane Nine of 1946, taken June 23, 1946, between double-header games

Darkness. Quiet. A sound of crackling, like a bonfire.

Mel Cole could only hear, not see. He wondered where he was. He wondered why he couldn't see. He tried to touch his eyes. He couldn't do that either.

"You've not survived," he heard a woman's voice say next to him. He turned towards the voice and suddenly could see a woman with kind eyes sitting next to him on the ground.

"Survived," he repeated, slowly.

"You've died," the spirit-soul said, kind eyes still.

"I'm dead," he said in response, as if in a trance. He tried to look around, but could see only her. She was like a glow of light, as she sat beside him there.

"The bus crashed," she said. "Many have died. Not just you. See? Look." She pointed towards the sound of crackling.

He turned towards where she pointed and now could see. A fire blazed the size of the bus. He saw men from the team standing, looking at the blaze. They stepped towards the bus, then away. There was no hope for anyone inside.

"Your body's in there," she said, pointing to the bus. "You were trapped in there. You tried, but you couldn't get out."

"So why am I over here if my body's in there?" he asked her.

"Your soul is here," she said. "With me."

"Okay," Mel said, dazed. "Dead?" She nodded. "You're sure?" he asked.

But even before he asked, he knew she was right. He could tell something was different. He was a body without a body, a voice without a voice. He realized that they had not even been speaking words, really – thought-words, more like.

"I'm sure," she said. "I'm sorry," she added, looking kindly at him in her white glow way.

He nodded. Thought of Mimi. The baby. No father for that baby, he thought. He would have cried, if he had eyes. Or tears. He could feel his heart cry, though.

"He'll be safe," the spirit-soul next to him said. "The baby will be loved. By you for one," she said, her glow of light lightening more as she smiled at him. "And by those around him. It will be hard, but he will be loved."

She looked out to the bus. "These men – they need your help," the spirit-soul said, gesturing outward. "Many have died, others will die soon. The rest will never forget." She turned and glowed at him, brightest yet. "They need your help, Mel Cole. Together, we will help them."

She led him towards the burning bus. Fire still shot into the air. She pointed to the handful of men standing in awe of the flames, helpless – Ben Geraghty, Gus Hallbourg among them. "These men live," she said. "They will survive."

Then she gestured into the dark. "Can you see these others?" she asked.

"What others?" Mel asked.

"The souls," she said. "The ones who have died with you. They're right here. In front of you."

He squinted into the darkness. He thought he saw someone – Freddie, maybe. "I don't know," he said, cautiously. "I don't know. What do they look like?"

"Like shadows, only more, and less – not dark," she said, trying to help him see.

He heard a moan then, and started to back away. "It's Vic," she said. "Come with me to him." She led Mel around the side of the bus – in an instant, they were there. Young Vic Picetti lay on a large, flat rock, in agony.

"Vic," Mel said, almost involuntarily. Levi stood there with him, still alive, his back to Mel and the spirit-soul.

"Vic will hear you, but not your words, at least not until he dies," the spirit-soul said.

"He's going to die?" Mel said.

"Yes," she answered.

"But we were sending him home, after this trip," Mel said, distressed. "Why do you think he will die?"

"Because it is already set," she said. "In a way, it's already happened. It won't happen for another hour. But in a way, it's already done." She shook her head as though that was not the important thing. "He needs you right now Mel. Stand by him. Talk to him. Tell him he's safe. Whatever you can say, say it to him." There was a sound of an ambulance. "Go with him in the ambulance," she said. "I'll find the others. Vic needs you right now, next to him." And then she was gone.

But Mel kept looking at Levi and Vic – both wounded, both still alive. Mel couldn't imagine what to do. If he were dead, how could he talk? And was he really dead? It couldn't be. He looked around the scene, as though it were a dream. He tried to wander towards the bus. Maybe if he walked to the bus, he'd wake up.... But each of his steps moved him nowhere. It was like he was fixed where he was – like a vertical piece of clear glass let him see the flames but prevented him from walking towards them....

He turned to look back towards Vic and Levi. He started to float that way instead.... He felt himself approach the two men almost against his will.... gingerly, even.... like a wisp of air....

Suddenly Levi spun around. Mel and Levi – there they were, face to face – with one face missing. Levi peered into the dark before him. Squinted. Took in a breath of air. Stared into the space where Mel stood, wavering in the night air.

"Mel," Levi said. He peered again. He moved his hand into Mel's unformed space. "Mel," Levi said again, this time sadly, his hand passing through the spirit of Mel. This jerked Mel out of air and into – something else. Something solid. Something formed. It was as though Levi had made him solid on the ground of his death. So that he could be formed in his lack of form. As though Levi had awakened him.

"Levi," Mel said, and took a step towards him. Past him. Towards Vic. "Help him," Mel heard the spirit-soul say again (from where, he didn't know).

So Mel and Levi stood side by side, watching over Vic. Mel stood still while Levi spoke softly, telling Vic he was a good boy and that his mother loved him. Levi started to sing – chant, more like, softly chant – but not in words that Mel understood....

Gus Hallbourg walked up, tears streaming. He took off his jacket – that beautiful leather jacket his mother had given him before he came to Spokane – and draped it across the Kid, to protect him from the cold, rainy night that descended upon them....

Now that Mel was next to Vic, he could see how bad his injuries were, how it would be impossible for the Kid to survive. As the ambulance arrived, Levi stayed by Vic's side and Mel stayed too. When the medics put Vic on a stretcher, Mel felt Levi brace himself to absorb some of the boy's pain (this Mel could feel but had not known – that Levi could do such a thing). Instinctively, Mel did the same. He followed Levi's lead. He would work with Levi to help Vic.

But when the drivers went to carry Vic up the steep mountainside, Levi couldn't go. His knee wouldn't work. The drivers went ahead, with Levi staying behind in his grief. Mel couldn't help Levi anymore. Whatever Mel did, he did on his own. As he stood with Levi to watch them go, he knew he had to follow. "Levi," Mel said (thought-said). "I'm here, Chief," he said. "Don't worry about Vic. I'll go with him."

Levi paused in his grief to look where Mel's spirit stood. He nodded. "Go," he said.

So it was Mel's turn to stand by Vic's side and tell him he was a good boy, that his mother loved him.... over and over, he said the words – thought-said them. And when Vic cried out in agony at any jostle up the slope, Mel could hardly bear it (oh Vic, I'm so sorry, you're safe, kid, you'll be okay). He patted towards Vic's shoulder, told him he was brave.... and when Vic died on the way to the hospital, Mel saw his soul emerge – like a shadow, only more (and less) than a shadow. Like a shadow of light.

"You've not survived," he said softly into the young man's white-shadow ear.

Vic turned towards Mel's voice. "Survived," Vic repeated, slowly....

Denny Spellecy, sports reporter, was ready to go home. There was no late night game to worry about. And it already was late. He could leave before the final edition deadline, if he wanted. But something held him in the newsroom. "Stay," he almost heard. I need to stay, is what he thought.

Soon it was after eight and still he shuffled papers, shuffled around, delaying his departure. He started looking through paperwork for the high school all-star team that he was in charge of organizing, a promotion with the Brooklyn Dodgers. That was a big project and just around the corner.

Jerry O'Neill, from the Associated Press, came from the AP room. "Denny?"

"What?" Denny said, turning around. Jerry just handed him a teletype report. It was from the AP operator in Seattle. Denny's face went white as he read. "State patrol says chartered bus has gone off road at Snoqualmie Pass," it read, "and that it may be Spokane baseball team. Please check club there soonest. Seattle."

"I better call Sam," Denny said, and started for the phone.

Jerry stopped him. "I already did. Sam thinks it's not our bus – that we would be over the pass by now. But he's going to make some calls." They heard the teletype machine start printing again. Jerry went to see what news it had. Simultaneously the phone rang.

"Newsroom," Denny said, as he picked up the phone. He put his head down, nodding. His reporter's hand took notes. "fire...

burning... five, maybe six... some too burned... Risk... Martinez... Cole?..." Denny stared at his notes. "This is terrible," he said to the person on the line. "I can't believe...." Paused. Listened more. Nodded into the phone. Took more notes.

Denny hung up. "It was Sam," he said to the newsmen who gathered around. "Five, most likely six dead, they're not even sure who, the bodies are so burned." He looked again at his notes. He had the names of the ones thought to be dead. He added in where each of the players were from. He knew these men, knew their hometowns, knew it just to write it down. Added "apparently" to the question-marked names ("Apparently dead," he wrote). Put a question mark by Vic Picetti's name – wounded, he wrote. "I've got head shots," he said to no one in particular, and left to go dig them out. He realized, as he looked through their bios, how each of the men on the list was just back from the war. All but young Vic was just back from the war.

Denny, too. Back in time to try to make things happen, like this all-star game he was working on. These men worked hard, like he did. They had followed their dream. Just to die? He shook his head at the thought and kept digging through his files.

The phone rang once more just as Denny found the photos of each of the six men. He handed the photos to the news editor and took the phone. He called up Dwight, Sam again. They were on their way down to the paper already. Denny sat. There was nothing to do. Then he sighed. There *was* one thing, he thought, as he went back to his desk to find a photograph of the Kid. Just in case.

"Hon?" Gus Hallbourg said, from a telephone in Ellensburg.
"Gus?" his wife said, half asleep.
"Hon," Gus started, his voice cracking.
"What's wrong?" Berta asked, waking herself up to hear him.
"The bus – it crashed, fell off the side of the hill."
Berta gasped. "Are you all right?"
"I'm fine, I'm fine. But the others."
"Is it Levi?"
"Levi's all right – he is. But the Kid ..." He told her of the jacket, and of climbing up the side of the hill, and of the bus driver going east who had offered him the ride to Ellensburg. Ma will be mad about the jacket, he said at the end.

"No, she won't," Berta said. "You did the right thing." It was the right thing to do, she murmured again as she turned on the light, waiting for him to arrive.

Sam and Dwight got to the newspaper building at the same time. Dwight had a book of names and phone numbers of relatives in case of emergencies. Sam first called the state patrol and the Seattle hospital to get more information. Then he called his daughter Joyce to have her start collecting the local wives at the Collins' home.

When all that was done, all that was left was the one thing he did not want to do. But they all said he had to do it. It had to come from the owner, they all said.

Still, Sam stalled. Where to start? He saw Bob James' name. "I met Bob's brother once," Sam said, musing. He talked of how Bill was a likeable sort, outgoing like Bob, a little more careful than their wild baserunner. It's a great thing when brothers are friends, Sam said. Then he was quiet, staring at the phone. He picked up the receiver. The operator clicked on. "Operator?" he said. "Get me Mr. W.T. James in Tempe, Arizona, telephone number ..."

The phone rang again. It was Joyce Collins. "Oh, Berta – Gus has died," Joyce said.

"What?" Berta said, astounded, confused. "But I just talked to him."

"What?" came the response. So Berta said what had happened.

Joyce was angry. "You should have called," she said, as if there were protocol to follow in times like this. Someone came and picked up Berta, taking her to the Collins' home where all the other wives were, as they all made phone calls home in the middle of the night.

"Mrs. Picetti?" Sam said.

"Yes?" Vic's mother said.

"There's been an accident," Sam said. "We don't know yet...."

This is how they learned that something may have happened. Though nothing was for sure. They huddled all night – Vic's mother, sister, baby brother and fiancee – without hearing another word and with no way to learn more, no matter how they tried to call the ballpark (where no one was) or the newspaper in San Francisco (where they couldn't get through).

· · ·

Denny took the phone call. This time it was for sure. On Vic. Denny wrote what the reporter was telling him – "This man is dead" (doc) ... "best player on club" (Pete Barisoff). Denny put down the phone and picked up the headshot of the Kid. He stared at it. Then he sighed and went to look at the page layout, to add in this last photo. He scanned the proofs.

"Where are the photos?" he asked.

"I didn't get any photos," the assistant said.

"Of the six players that died," Denny said. "There's a seventh to add." The assistant shrugged. Denny shook his head in disbelief, then crossed the room to the news editor.

"What about the photos?" Denny said.

"We don't have time to make room for photos, Denny," the news editor said. "We're on deadline. There's just not time."

"So make time," Denny said. He thought of Sam and Dwight, making telephone calls upstairs in the AP office. "This is not a choice. This is not a decision that doesn't matter." He squared his jaw. "This paper can't go out without these photographs in it. It's not right. You need their faces. There's no other choice." He paused. "They're *dead*."

His words seemed to shock the news editor into action, and made him go to the backshop. "Hold on," the news editor shouted, then picked up the paper's third edition – the last edition of the press before they had heard. He thumbed through the paper, to the inside page where the story continued. He looked it over. "Take this and this out," he said. "Run the photos across the top."

A pause in the action....

"Sit down, Denny," someone said. "Take a break." But if he did, he would cry, Denny thought. Still, he walked down the hall to a room where no one was. Sat down. Stared. And kept his face hidden from view.

Chaos. Anxiety. Confusion. Grief.

These were the senses rushing through him.

Some were what Mel felt. Most came from those around him.

His first urge was to shake off what wasn't his. But then he remembered the spirit-soul's words: "These men – they need your help."

It was true. They did. And he was their manager. He would not let them down.

Mostly it seemed they needed his reassurance. Like he had done for Vic. Words didn't matter. Senses did. So he walked amongst them to help them feel safe.

First he walked amongst the dead. He could see them now. Their shadow forms became clearer as that night wore on. They had all collected at the hospital, with the living part of the team. Stood in the hallways, wandered through....

There were the three Bobs. There was Bob James, so full of life in life, now full of life in death. The man who raced past second on well-hit doubles connected up quickly to Mel and was there to help, he said. But he was also frantic for his family, his brother Bill mostly, and disappeared often that night to be with them (and then bounced back to stand next to Mel)....

There was Bob Paterson, the center fielder to take over from Dwight, a quieter man, more anxious than sad in death, it seemed. He was off to himself a bit, dazed a little, but alert enough, and connected to them. He left to see his wife, then came back to see the team....

And there was Bob Kinnaman, a veteran in life, a mainstay in death. He spent the night at George Lyden's bedside as the young pitcher groaned in pain from his horrible, horrible burns and injuries....

"I'll be by George if you need me," Kinnaman said. Mel nodded. Both knew that this boy would be the eighth to die, would join them as a light shadow soon.

"But what about your folks?" Mel said.

Just then, Bob James appeared. "I'll sit with him, Bob," he said. "You go check on your folks."

Kinnaman shook his head no. "I know my dad," he said. "If he knew all this, he would want me to sit with George while he ... he dies. Besides, my parents are together. They'll comfort each other." He looked down. "Besides," he said again, moving closer to the young pitcher groaning on the bed, "it's my fault, really, all this." He paused. "I'm the one who gave him hope for his game...."

Bob James stayed for awhile then, not to take his friend's place but to give him strength as the night wore on.

And then there was the other George. Risk. Their college kid. So sure of himself, but with his moments of superstition (with three two-dollar bills in his wallet with the corners torn off for luck). Off to himself, in life – off to himself now, in death. His family lived south of Seattle. His wife Marjie was in Spokane. He had left to be near them, bounce between them. But his soul seemed lost – like they all were, only him more than most....

"Hold his soul close," the spirit-soul said – why, she didn't say – so Mel kept finding Risk and bringing him back for a moment or two. "Just be with me George," he would say. "I'd appreciate the company...."

Then there was quiet Freddie Martinez – quieter now, as though English was beyond him. Too much shock. He wasn't there much that night. Mostly he was gone to be with his wife. She was inconsolable. And there was that baby she carried....

And finally, Vic. The Kid. Wretched. Confused. Disconnected. How to help him, how to hold him together....

"Don't lose him," the spirit-soul said. "Don't let him stray from your light too far." So Mel checked in often on the boy whose homesick heart would have been at least partially healed had they made it through to Bremerton.

Once Mel had found the dead, he started to walk amongst those who survived. Who barely survived. George Lyden and at least one more would not pull through, the spirit-soul had told him. And no one – not one of them – would be the same again. Something had happened to change everything for always. And all of them needed him now, she said. So he walked on through, to each bed, spoke encouragement and solace into each of the players still living. For, throughout his life and now, in the end, this was a man of heart. And it was in his heart to help his men.

The Chief heard him best. Could talk to him too, that Mel knew. Maybe it was in Levi's Indian blood to hear from the beyond, but he could tell that Levi felt him every time he was around. Ben Geraghty, too, seemed to sense it when Mel stood by him. Mel didn't know if it helped, to speak into these men, to speak into the Chief, who was despondent and grieved every time Mel was near. But the spirit-soul said it would help, so he did what she said.

Many times that first night, Mel wanted to die again, this time for good – so that he went into nothingness, not this in-between state. In those moments, the spirit-soul was instantly at his side, sensing his despair, telling him to collapse for a moment while reminding him of the tasks at hand. They need you, they need you, more now than before, more in this moment than they ever will, she said to him as his heart wept.

At one of the points when he was thinking of his wife, Mel felt himself whisked to Mimi's side as she sat in their house with the big basement room. He sat by Mimi's side and try to brush back her hair, and watched her rub her belly with both hands, as she thought of their child without him. She cried and cried as she sat alone, which was what she believed she was. "I love you," he said, washing her with his heart.... And then he was whisked back again, to the halls of the hospital, where souls gathered to sort through chaos, where he had no time left but to think of them.

The spirit-soul stood with him that night, almost always and always when he asked her to. In an instant, she would be there. "How is Mimi?" he asked her as the sun started to rise, as he stood in the hospital halls.

"They've gathered the women together," the spirit-soul responded, and he knew she meant the team.

"I don't know what I'm doing," he said to her then. "I know you say these men need me, but for what? Why? And how to help?"

"Just move one step at a time," she said. "Each step will guide you to the next. Just move one step at a time." So he did.

It was 6 a.m. when the telephone rang. It was Grace's cousin, waking her up, telling her something may have happened to Chris, something was on the radio. Grace raced down the steps of her parents' townhome as fast as her pregnant body would let her, to the San Francisco Chronicle's metal newspaper stand on the street corner below. She stood there in her nightgown, ready to give birth, staring at the headline, sobbing, gasping for air, saying over and over, oh no, oh no....

On the other side of town, in the very same moments, Betty told Vic's mother to stay by the phone while Betty walked the three blocks by herself to the grocery store where she knew there was a newspaper rack.

The headlines said it all. Vic Picetti was dead.

The early editions of The Spokesman-Review for June 25, 1946 did not mention the accident because they were printed before the editors knew what had happened. Those early editions were printed at 7 and 8 p.m. the night before, and the crash didn't happen until right after eight.

It wasn't until the fourth edition that the news surfaced. The headline ran across the entire top of the front page. Banner headlines, they are called.

"7 MEMBERS OF SPOKANE BALL TEAM KILLED IN STAGE CRASH"

It was perfunctory, as stories go. The newsmen knew so little, had so little time to gather information in time to make the paper's next edition. The paper showed how they were not even sure that they had the right names to list as the dead:

Six bodies were found at the spot where the bus hurtled down a precipitous embankment and burned. One died of injuries before reaching a Seattle hospital.

List of Dead

The identified dead were:

George C. Risk, an infielder from Hillsboro, Ore.; Frederick T. Martinez, an infielder from San Diego; Vic Picetti, first baseman from San Francisco who formerly played with Oakland. He died en route to the hospital.

Others Listed Killed

The four other dead apparently were: Manager Mel Cole of Wenatchee, Wash.; Bob Kinnaman, a pitcher from Brooklyn, Wash.; Outfielder Bob James of Tempe, Ariz., and Outfielder Bob Paterson of San Francisco.

They were all names dear to the people from Spokane – names that they had been calling out from the stands for weeks. They knew that George Risk had made a heck of catch early on in the season (back before he returned to shortstop), snagging the ball off the outfield fence, saving the team from a near grand slam. They knew Freddie Martinez initially was called an outfielder, then an infielder, and then became the guy who could play either. They knew Bob James was the one too enthusiastic to keep sane in his base running. They knew Bob Paterson was the guy who had to fill the shoes of Dwight Aden. Their hearts ached to see Bob Kinnaman's name – a veteran pitcher, he had played for the Indians even before the war, always with such a strong grin, laugh. And to have the young manager Mel Cole dead too.... He had done well, this young man who had stepped in at the last minute. He had been tough, the readers thought, the morning of the 25th, as they read the paper and read Mel's name and remembered how he had been ousted from a game so recently for standing up to the ump.

And then there was the youngest on the team, first baseman Vic Picetti, their rising star. The paper recorded the proclamation of his death: "The stretchers were taken from the ambulances and rolled into the hospital emergency ward. A doctor made a quick inspection. 'This man is dead,' he said." And it recorded pitcher Pete Barisoff, "as tears streaked his begrimed face," saying, "'It's Vic, the best player on the club....'"

Photos of the seven dead spanned across the top of page seven. Headshots. Grinning faces, serious faces, faces caught in action, no pose. Every kind of photo spanned the top of the page. Not a banner headline – just so many photos that they stretched that far. It caught people's breaths, throughout Spokane, to see these faces of men from the field. Good men. Gone. Gone for good.

The paper, with the help of The Associated Press, had interviews with some of the survivors. "I'm lucky to be alive," at least two of them said. Ben Geraghty, second baseman, said it enough to be quoted in the paper as saying it twice. "I guess I'm pretty lucky," they quoted him, and then: "'I've got a wife and three kids in Spokane,' he said. 'I guess I'm pretty lucky to come out alive.'"

Pitcher Gus Hallbourg had the most detailed quotes about the accident:

> "I turned to Bob Kinnaman and said, 'This would be a hell of a place to go over, wouldn't it?' I turned back and we were going through the fence. The bus caught fire almost right away as it rolled down. It must have been about 500 feet down. You could see the rocks of the hillside flying past as we rolled. I rode her clear to the bottom. I guess I was knocked unconscious for a bit when we landed. When I came to, the inside of the bus was all flames. I dove out through a window." He said rescuers from the highway helped him back up the steep slope and "when I left the bus it was just ashes."

Photos of the bus surfaced a day later. All that was left was a shell.

It was 8 a.m. now, the next day. Denny Spellecy thought back to how he had sat with Sam and Dwight in the newsroom as they had awaited any news, and how Sam had started making phone calls even before they had known all the information for sure.

"They say George Lyden is in the worst shape of the ... the ones still alive," Denny remembered Sam saying as the night wore on.

"Then we got to get his wife there as fast as we can," Dwight had said.

"I'll call," Sam had said, as he traced the list with his finger until he found the Lyden number. "Betty? Sam Collins. Sorry to call so late.... Can you hear me all right? Betty? Betty, there's been an accident...."

And so it had gone.

Sam was worn out. So was Dwight. They had been working non-stop. Getting family to Seattle. Arranging for babysitters. Trying to find the right person to speak to Freddie Martinez's wife – someone who spoke Spanish (it was not a time to speak English to her). For-getting – or not knowing where – to contact Grace Hartje, the new player's wife, who, unbeknownst to them, was now chartering a ride on a cargo plane on her own to get to Seattle as soon as possible, regardless of her doctor's advice. Trying to reach Dutch Anderson, their trainer, before he learned about the crash from the newspaper he would undoubtedly read as he traveled to join back up with the team he expected to see in Bremerton....

It was as if there was no end. And yet it was better than standing still. Because if they stopped, they would think. And they did not want to think.

The spirit-soul stood with them, watching them work, feeling their chaos, knowing their grief, knowing the grief that was yet to come, whispering thoughts into them. She had failed at helping them contact Grace, though she had tried....

"I should go, I should go," Sam had kept saying about Seattle, and the hospital where the ball players lay.

"Stay here," Dwight had said, knowing Sam was just out of the hospital himself, knowing his health was in jeopardy from the past hours. "I'll go with Ken," he said, meaning Ken Hunter, their publicity manager. "Ken can talk to the press. We'll tell the team that you're making arrangements."

That satisfied Sam. "Tell them we're doing all we can here," he had said.

As he got to the hospital, Dwight took a deep breath. He didn't know, really, what they would find. He knew George Lyden, Chris Hartje and pitcher Dick Powers were thought to be the worst off. Dick, the doctors said, had broken his neck. Chris – Chris was covered with burns, under constant care, hardly could breathe, his breath stolen by the extent of his burns. George Lyden – well, they had told him they did not think that George would survive. He was unconscious.

Otherwise, though, Dwight didn't know what to expect. And who could? What could ever have prepared him – anyone – for this? Not even the war could have prepared him. At least in the war, you expect death.

Mel's soul stood at the hospital's entryway, waiting for him. Here was the man who had given Mel his chance. Had believed in him. Had seen a way to help him form this team.

"This way, Dwight," Mel said, speaking into him, guiding him forward.

Dwight sighed and walked through the hospital doors. He talked to doctors. Nodded. Walked to each bed. Dick was in and out of consciousness, Ben Geraghty told him, as Ben lay with a "V" stitched in his forehead, following the line of the gash that had almost taken off the top of his head. "I told him he scalped me," Ben said of Levi as Levi shook Dwight's hand. Dwight was just glad to see both men alive. It's just like how it was in the war, he thought as he wandered from bed to bed, checking in on each man.

Dwight walked up to Chris Hartje's bed. He was ill prepared for what he saw. Chris was completely bandaged up, scarcely breathing, tubes everywhere.

"Hello, Chris," he said. "It's Dwight Aden, the business manager," he said to the man lying there.

"'Lo," Chris said, weakly.

"How are you doing?" Dwight asked, hated to ask.

Chris nodded. "I'll be out of here in two or three days," he said. (Don't you worry, I'll not be long in this bed, he seemed to want to say.)

• • •

It was early morning by the time Dutch had gotten onto the ferry to cross over to Bremerton from Seattle. What an exhausting night, he thought, as he stretched his muscles from his all-night train ride and wondered how late it had been before the team had gotten to Bremerton the night before. He chuckled at his aches and pains and wondered what kind of team trainer that made him, to be so creaky himself. He stretched again, rubbed his eyes, and then remembered that he had bought a newspaper right before getting on the ferry to read during the ride over. He casually reached down, pulled the paper out of his bag, and opened it up to the front page.

Betty Lyden cried softly as she stood in the Seattle hospital. She had come with George's mother. She had left the two young boys back at home, with her mother. They shouldn't see their father like this. She wished she didn't have to, herself.

And now it didn't matter. He was gone. She sat down on a chair there in the hallway. Any chair would do. She was numb. She could hardly breathe.

Some of the souls sat next to her as she cried, in that moment by herself. "We don't know what to do," Mel said. "Send her love," the spirit-soul said.

So that is what they did. They sat beside Betty as she cried, and filled their senses with a sense of love.

"GEORGE LYDEN EIGHTH BUS CRASH FATALITY" was the newspaper's headline the next day, June 26th. It had his photo, too.

> George Lyden, 22-year-old right-handed pitcher from Tensed, Idaho, was the eighth victim in the crash and fire of a chartered bus carrying the Spokane Indian baseball team to Bremerton Monday night. Sixteen hours after the tragedy, Lyden succumbed to severe head injuries and burns while in a Seattle hospital.

There was more in the article: about who survived and how they were; about who had died on the 24th, listing their names for a second day, this time being able to confirm that they knew for sure that these were the dead men; about who was helping in the effort to

salvage the lives of the still-living – "the best doctors and brain spe-
cialists of Seattle have been obtained to treat the others injured."

There was just nothing more in the article about George Lyden.
He was dead.

But the Spokane fans knew. They remembered that George had
been doing a great job at relief. That he was so good that he had won
a starting berth. And that that would have be the last time he played.
Yes, on June 26th, as they read the headline about his dying on June
25th, they realized that they had gone to the stadium on June 23rd
knowing it was his first start, but not knowing it was his last. They
remembered, too, how they had cheered that day while his pitching
was strong; how he had lost a little edge at the end; how they had left
the game thinking he had done a pretty decent job for his first start.
At least he made it through to the ninth, they remembered they had
said to each other. And he'll do better next time, they remembered
saying, as they graciously reserved opinion until later about whether
he could last as a starter.

So even though the paper on the 26th had said no more about
George Lyden, the fans reading the paper knew more. And they knew
that now they would never know how he would do in his next start.

Dutch stumbled around the hospital, trying to find his teammates. Ultimately he made it to Chris' room and stood in shock at
how Chris looked.

"Chris," Dutch said, as all his frantic emotions drained away into
the quiet stillness of the hospital room. "It's Dutch, Chris."

"Clothes," Chris said in near whisper. He gestured towards the
door in the direction of the nurses' station. "Need my clothes," he
said.

"You just take care of yourself," Dutch said. "Don't you worry
about your clothes."

"Need 'em when I go," Chris said. "Be outta here in a coupla
days."

"Where to?" the cabbie said.

"I don't know," Grace answered, as she got into the taxi idling at
the airport curb. "All I know is, my husband – " Her voice caught.
She tried again. "He plays ball. In Spokane. The bus crashed...."
She couldn't say any more.

"Oh," the driver said, realizing what she meant. "Yes, ma'am.
Yes. I know it. I do know of it. I think they took all them players to

Seattle Hospital. Or Harborview. Harborview, I think. I know they did. We'll take you there. You just sit back, now. Don't you worry. I know where you have to go."

Grace fell back into her seat then, trusting him to know the way.

One more would die, the spirit-soul told Mel. That's what she said, so that's what he knew.

"He doesn't want to leave," Mel said to the spirit-soul, hours later.

She nodded. "Talk to him," she said. "Stand by him. Talk to him. Wait for him to see you."

Mel did as she said. He stood with Chris. He listened to Chris and his young wife.

"I'm sorry," Chris said to Grace once more. "I shoulda –"

"Stop," Grace said back as she sat as close to him as she could.

"I wish I'd come home," Chris whispered. "Never shoulda – Spokane."

"Don't talk. Save your strength," Grace said, putting her hand next to his head.

"Now," the spirit-soul said into Mel.

"Chris," Mel said.

Chris heard him. He looked over Grace's shoulder, where Mel stood. "Mel," Chris said.

"I didn't survive, Chris," Mel said kindly, just as Grace said, "Oh, Chris, Mel's died." Chris nodded.

"Come with me," Mel said, and the light around him shone. "It's time to go," he said, reaching out his hand to the badly burned man.

Chris shook his head no. I won't die, Mel heard him think. I can't. Grace ... the baby....

Mel turned to the spirit-soul right behind him. He didn't know what to do. Do I have to tell him to die? he thought to her. I can't do this, Mel thought. But the spirit-soul whispered into him. He nodded, and turned back to the man in the bed who said he wouldn't die.

"We need you here," Mel said, "on this side. Vic's in bad shape – he died too, but he's so young, Chris, he misses his family.... He needs our help. He needs *your* help. You've talked to him. You know him. You can help me help him."

Still Chris shook his head no. Mel nodded yes. "We need your help," he said. "The most the Kid can remember right now is his conversation with you, on the bus ride over. Maybe if you talk to him, he can hear you." He steeled himself, and started again. "But you can't talk to him on the side of the living. We need you on this side for you to be able to help." Mel paused. "And you can't survive. You cannot survive, Christian Hartje. It's now, or two hours from now, or two days from now, but you cannot survive." He waited. "And we need you now."

Then Chris sighed. It was his final breath alive.

The next day, the headline ran: "CATCHER HARTJE NINTH BUS DEATH."

> SEATTLE, June 26 (AP)—Christian Hartje, 30-year-old catcher on Spokane's Western International League baseball team, died tonight in a Seattle hospital....
>
> Six players were killed outright in the crash. One died en route to the hospital, and Hartje was the second to die in a hospital.... Hartje suffered deep burns over his entire body and underwent constant blood and fluid transfusions in an effort to save his life.
>
> Mrs. Hartje arrived in Seattle Tuesday night by air from San Francisco in a chartered plane. She has been at the bedside of her husband since.

The "HARTJE DEAD" headline was not in the newspaper's first edition. That first headline had read: "TWO BUS CRASH VICTIMS WORSE: Fear Felt For Life Of Dick Powers And Chris Hartje." The first paragraph of the earlier story foretold what then happened a few hours later: "Spokane Catcher Chris Hartje, 30, injured and badly burned in the bus crash Monday night ... was reported to be worse yesterday afternoon. Hospital attendants at Seattle said he would not live through the night."

Two editions later, he no longer was Chris. It was Christian, in death.

He'd been optioned to the Spokane Indians just nine days before the crash. He had played his first game five days before, on June 19th. They had loved him then. "Hartje Wins Fans," the subheadline had read. "Hartje Wins Hearts," it should have read.

Nine days. He had gotten to Spokane just in time to die.

He had been injured during the double-header on the 23rd, the newspaper said, but not injured enough to get bumped from the ride over Snoqualmie Pass on the 24th. No doubt he had protested any delay in his playing, is what Spokane thought. The knee's okay, was what fans knew he would have said. The knee's fine. He was a man back from the war who had played in the majors long enough to know he wanted to get back there. I can make the trip to Bremerton, they knew he would have said. The knee will be fine.

Later the newspaper ran his photo. "The body of Christian Hartje, ninth member of the Spokane Indians baseball team to die as a result of the tragic bus accident Monday, yesterday was taken from Seattle to San Francisco, where funeral plans will be announced," the caption read. "Hartje, former Brooklyn Dodgers catcher, had just joined the Spokane squad."

Nine dead. It took three days for nine to die.

An early view of the baseball field at Natatorium Park, out by the river.
Photo courtesy Northwest Museum of Arts and Culture (L97-15.39)

A view of the baseball fields and grandstand at Old Nat Park.

The entry gate before a baseball game
out at Old Nat Park in the early days.

SPOKANE, WASH.

FIRE WIPES OUT
BIG GRANDSTAND

Natatorium Park Scene
of Spectacle on the
Fourth.

THREE MEN HURT

Ball Players Caught in Rooms,
Have Difficulty in
Escaping.

FIREWORKS THE CAUSE

Twenty Thousand Persons See
Flames Raze Structure on Which
Loss Will Reach $6500.

Fire destroyed the grandstand at
Natatorium park at 6 o'clock last evening, causing a loss of $6500. Twenty
thousand persons witnessed the spectacle. To a small boy and a fire-
cracker is the destruction attributed
by the park management. The ball
game had ended five minutes before
and the 2000 spectators had made their
exit in safety when the flames started.
Had the fire broken out 10 minutes
earlier hundreds would have inevitably
been burned or trampled to death.
Twenty ballplayers were caught in
the dressing room under the north
end of the grandstand and only man-
aged to escape with their lives by sac-
rificing clothing and valuables and
running at top speed half clad. Several were severely burned. The injured:
W. F. Conner, president of the City
league, severely burned about head,
neck and hands.
Peter Parks, both hands severely
burned.
Harry Dunkle, back blistered by
heat.
In estimating the aggregate loss, the
following items are considered: Grandstand and fence, $5800; fireworks, $150;
personal effects of ball players, $550.
Spreads With Incredible Speed.
With incredible speed the flames
licked up the pine structure. So fast
did the tongues of fire leap from section to section that President Con-

Article dated
July 5, 1906

Photos courtesy Northwest Museum of Arts and Culture
(L89-27, L97-63.163)

Photo of Levi McCormack, printed in
the newspaper as the season began

Cadinha to Hurl Tonight's Opener

Milt Cadinha was Manager Mel Cole's selection to handle the
hurling job for the Spokane Indians in tonight's opener against
Vancouver. Cadinha, a stocky right-hander who was one of
Tacoma's mainstays before the war, went to Hawaii with the
San Francisco Seals for spring training and is in top condition.

Indian Stickmen Ready for Season Opener Tonight

They expect the fences at Ferris field to be
rattling with base hits tonight when the Spokane Indians open the 1946 Western International league season against the Vancouver
Capilanos and this quintet of Indians may do
most of the "rattling." Three of these heavy
hitters will be in the outfield when "play ball"
sounds and all have the reputation of being
long-ball hitters. Shown, left to right, are Spokane fans' favorite left fielder, Levi McCormack, George Risk, Bob James, Babe Jensen
and Bob Peterson.

Spokane Baseball Fans Attend Season's Opener

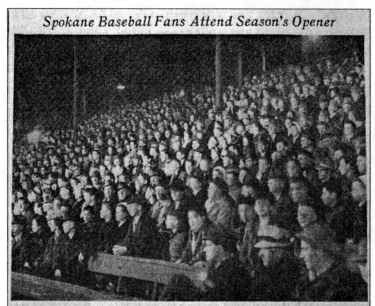

This is part of the crowd of more than 4000 persons who attended the opening of Spokane's baseball season at Ferris field last night to see the Spokane Indians play the Vancouver Capilanos. The Spokane team won, 5 to 0. In spite of transportation difficulties and the chilly night turnout was good for the season's opening baseball contest.

Paterson Provides Indians' Power

Big Bob Patterson provided the power at the plate for Spokane in the season's opener at Ferris field last night, banging out a double in the first inning to drive in two runs. Here he is shown pulling into third base in the first frame. He later scored as he and Levi McCormack pulled a double steal.

Players peer out of the Indians dugout in 1940. Pitcher
Bob Kinnaman is one of those pictured.

Photo courtesy Northwest Museum Arts and Culture (L86-640.17)

Dwight Aden

Photo courtesy Dwight Aden, Sr.

64TH YEAR. NO. 42   TUESDAY MORNING,   JUNE 25, 1946.   PRICE FIVE CENTS   SPOKANE, WASH.

7 MEMBERS OF SPOKANE BALL TEAM KILLED IN STAGE CRASH

Conferees Slash Powers of OPA but Vote Year's Extension

Chartered Bus Plunges Off
Snoqualmie Pass Grade;
Several Are Hurt.

Baseball Players Who Were Killed in Tragic Bus Crash Pictured

FRED MARTINEZ. — GEORGE RISK. — BOB KINNAMAN. — VIC PICETTI. — MEL COLE. — BOB JAMES. — BOB PATTERSON.

90

Eighth Victim

The death of George Lyden, Spokane pitcher, raised to eight the toll of dead in the tragic wreck of the Indians' Bremerton-bound bus. Lyden succumbed yesterday afternoon to injuries sustained in the crash.

Chris Hartje

The body of Christian Hartje, ninth member of the Spokane Indians baseball team to die as a result of the tragic bus accident Monday, yesterday was taken from Seattle to San Francisco, where funeral plans will be announced. Hartje, former Brooklyn Dodgers catcher, had just joined the Spokane squad. (Photo: Brooklyn Eagle.)

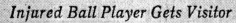

Injured Ball Player Gets Visitor

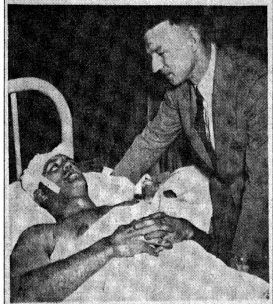

Pitcher Irv Konopka gets a visit from Dwight Aden, business manager of the Spokane Indians, as he lies in bed at Harborview hospital, Seattle, recovering from injuries suffered in the tragic crash of the team's Bremerton-bound chartered bus Monday night. Konopka was at first thought to have sustained a broken neck, but X-rays yesterday did not show any fractures.

Spokane Ball Team's Bus After Crash That Cost Lives of Eight

Eight members of the Spokane Indians baseball club lost their lives and seven others were injured when the chartered bus in which they were driving to Bremerton plunged off Snoqualmie pass highway Monday night. The machine tumbled 300 feet down an embankment and caught fire. The bus struck boulders in the foreground after tearing out guard rail. (AP wirephoto.)

Ben Geraghty Went Out Window

Ben Geraghty, Indians' infielder, went through a window and took the frame with him as the ball club's bus plunged off a cliff on Snoqualmie pass. His fortunate dive saved him from more serious injury than the head cuts he sustained. Geraghty, 31, was a former player of Sacramento and Indianapolis teams. He is married and the father of three children. (AP photo.)

Escaped Crash

Jack Lohrke, Spokane third baseman, had left the ill-fated Indians' bus at Ellensburg where he was caught by a telephone call from Sam W. Collins notifying him he had been recalled to the San Diego club of the Pacific Coast league. He was safe in Spokane last night.

Dwight Aden's wife Esther accepting a check
for $2,500 from Bing Crosby.

Photo courtesy Dwight Aden, Sr.

The players in the memorial game signed the cover
of this copy of the memorial game program.

Photo courtesy Northwest Museum of Arts and Culture

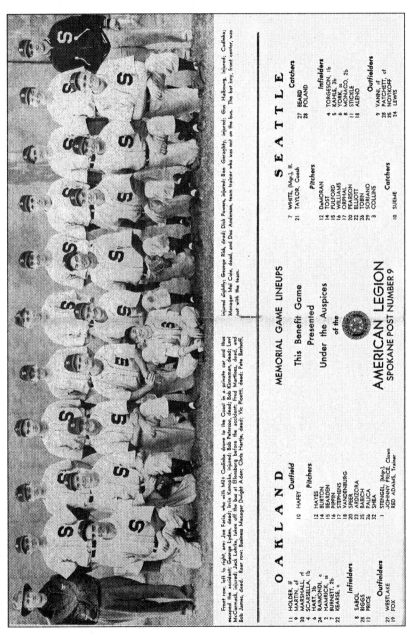

Front row, left to right, are: Joe Faria, who with Milt Cadinha drove to the Coast in a private car and thus escaped the accident; George Lydum, dead; Irvin Konopka, injured; Bob Peterson, dead; Bob Kimmaman, dead; Levi McCormack, injured; Jack LaVelle, taken off the bus at Ellensburg before the accident; Fred Martinez, dead; and Bob James, dead. Rear row: Business Manager Dwight Aden; Chris Hartle, dead; Vic Picetti, dead; Pete Barisoff.

injured slightly; George Risk, dead; Dick Powers, injured; Ben Geraghty, injured; Gus Hallbourg, injured; Cadinha; Manager Mel Cole, dead, and Doc Anderson, team trainer who was not on the bus. The bat boy, front center, was not with the team.

OAKLAND		SEATTLE	
		7 WHITE, (Mgr.), lf	
	Outfield	21 TAYLOR, Coach	
11 HOLDER, lf			Catchers
9 MARTIN, cf	10 HAFEY		27 BEARD
30 MARSHALL, rf			28 POLAND
4 SCARSELLA, 1b	Pitchers		
6 HART, 3b			Infielders
24 RAIMONDI, c	12 HAYES		4 TORGESON, 1b
2 HAMRICK, ss	14 BURTON		5 KAHLE, 3b
7 BURNETT, 2b	15 BEARDEN		6 YORK, ss
22 KEARSE, c	16 PIPPIN		8 MONACO, 2b
	17 VANDENBURG		18 ALENO
Infielders	18 VANDENBURG		
	20 SPEER		
8 SABOL	23 ARDIZORA		
28 BIGGS	25 BARICH		
13 PRICE	26 PALICA		
	32 SHEA		
Outfielders			
	1 STENGEL, (Mgr.), Clown		
27 WESTLAKE	JOHNNY PRICE, Clown		
19 FOX	RED ADAMS, Trainer		

MEMORIAL GAME LINEUPS

This Benefit Game
Presented

Under the Auspices

of the

AMERICAN LEGION

SPOKANE POST NUMBER 9

Pitchers		Outfielders	
12 DeMORAN		9 VANNI, rf	
14 TOST		28 PATCHETT, cf	
15 PULFORD		25 NOVIKOFF	
16 WILLIAMS		24 LEWIS	
17 ORPHAL			
22 PEARSON			
22 ELLIOTT			
26 TOBIN			
29 SORIANO		Catchers	
3 COLLINS		10 SUEME	

Taken from middle of memorial game program

95

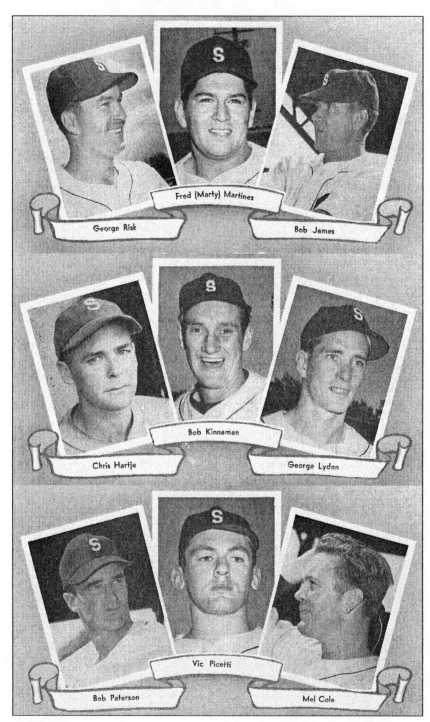

Photos in the memorial game program of the nine men who died.

Star of last night's Ferris field ceremonies honoring him, Levi (Chief) McCormack, popular veteran of the Spokane Indians baseball team, receives a gold baseball from Robert B. | Abel, Tacoma, president of the Western International league, as Spokane's Mayor Arthur Meehan looks on. In the foreground is new luggage, one of the gifts showered on the "Chief."

The photograph of Ben Geraghty with his
cap on backwards, see Afterword.

Photo courtesy Dwight Aden, Sr.

Two-Alarm Fire at Ferris Field Destroys Grandstand, Leaving Spokane Indians Homeless

Firemen last night responded to two alarms to battle a blaze at Ferris field that burned the grandstands to the ground and invaded the bleachers. Roof-like timbers were still flaming when this picture was taken from just beyond the infield near third base. Firemen to the right were fighting the fire and wetting down the bleachers in an attempt to save one of the sections. The goal line marker for high school football games, which took over the field after the Western International league baseball season ended, is in the foreground. The fire stripped the city of its last large outdoor sports arena.

October 30, 1948

PART 4

Promises

The Bastard had made her this promise in the month before her capture: no matter what else happened, he would not let her die alone. He knew the only things she feared were dying by fire and dying alone. And he knew she had visions of the fire. So he knew she would die by it, and he knew that she knew. Often he would wake up with the fear of her death caught in his throat. His promise was as much for himself as it was for her – as if to say, no matter what else, now I know I will always see her one last time.

They did all they could to rescue her in those months that she was held prisoner in Rouen. He had led one of the efforts; La Hire had led the other two. But their raid attempts failed. They had run out of time to try again.

The morning she was to die, he dressed up in disguise as a monk (brown with brown hood). He and Friar Isambard would both be killed if they were caught sneaking him into the city. But no one noticed. They were too busy getting ready to set her on fire to notice a royal-blooded general in paupers' clothes.

He found his way to the front of the crowd, right in front of the stake. Later they came with her, tied her to it. Friar Isambard was now on the platform with the executioners, holding the cross up for her, trying to show her that the general stood right below. At first she didn't see him, but the friar used the cross to gesture in his direction, and then she saw. And knew it was him. His brown hood covered much of his face, but she could see his eyes. Quick-thinking, even in the jaws of death, she asked the friar to step down from the platform to keep himself safe from the flames. As if reading her mind, the Bastard pulled the friar to him, took the cross, and held it close to his own face. Now she could look into his eyes as she looked at the cross.

Bishop Cauchon, who had orchestrated her trial and execution, came one last time to tell her to repent. "I die through you," she said, looking beyond the priest to the nobleman below. He nodded. Yes. I am here. Die through me.

The fire started to swirl up. Suddenly it was all he could do to keep from jumping on the platform and doing something, anything to delay her death. She held his gaze though, and was his strength. They could not stop this fate.

Then the flames crackled into a bonfire. And she burned. He stood and watched through to the end. Even as her ashes fell upon his face and melded into his skin, his eyes never strayed. He had come to fulfill a promise. He stayed until there was no more promise left to fulfill.

Owner Reads Messages of Condolence

Sam W. Collins, owner of the Spokane Indians, defied his doctor's orders to come down to the Spokane Baseball club offices in the Empire State building yesterday, to read the many messages of sympathy and offers of aid that poured in from all sections of the country. Upon Mr. Collins' shoulders rested the burden of responsibility for caring for members of the dead players' grief-stricken families.

The newspaper could not capture what happened to the team and the town in the aftermath. The disaster was too awful.

It did try. It tried by quoting men who were trying to use words to describe the indescribable. "This horrible accident is so terrible that I am unable to make a statement at this time," was one quote, from Robert Abel, president of the Western International Baseball League, of which the Spokane team was a part. "I have often wondered just what would happen to the league if such an accident should happen."

Another quote came from Trail, B.C., Canada, Senior Baseball Club: "Please convey to the management, the bereaved ones and the remaining members of the Spokane Indians, our deepest sympathy for the disastrous fate of their teammates. It is with regret that we learned of the accident which befell them. Ever sportsmen, their actions on the diamond will never be forgotten by the members of our club, by their many fans and by those on this side of the border who were fortunate enough to see them in action. Our deepest sympathy."

Denny Spellecy was in awe of the messages that poured into the newsroom. They came from everywhere. This was not about Spokane. This was not about baseball. It was not even about tragedy or the death of hopes. Perhaps it was about grief. And the spirits of these men. Why would God take the lives of men who never gave up?

The paper tried, too, by giving details. Somehow in times of disaster, bare facts give comfort. As though knowing "what" will somehow convert into knowing "why." So in the same way that it had tried, preseason, to give every detail it could (as it knew its readers wanted and needed), the newspaper provided what it could in the days following the accident (only these were facts from yesterday rather than words for tomorrow).

There were the details of the crash itself. "The accident occurred at 8 p.m. Monday evening four miles west of the summit in Snoqualmie Pass," the paper reported on June 26th, the second day of headlines – the day the report came out about George Lyden's death. "The Washington Motor Coach company bus transporting the 15 members to Bremerton plunged down a 500-foot embankment when forced to the side to avoid an oncoming vehicle."

There were updates on the still-living players. Pitcher Dick Powers and catcher Irv Konopka appeared to have head and neck injuries. Dick Powers' injury left him bedridden; Irv Konopka's injury turned out to be just his shoulder and he was soon discharged. Second baseman Ben Geraghty had had his head sliced open:

> "I was thrown right out a window as the bus turned over. I took the window frame right with me. I remember flying out the window, but I must have been knocked out because I don't remember landing. When I came to, I had lost a lot of blood and felt pretty weak but I got up on my feet and walked back up that hill. I don't remember about the wreck right now; I just know I went back up that hill."

A picture ran of the perfect "V" of a bandage Geraghty had on the top of his head, covering the perfect "V" of a slice he had received at the top of his scalp when pouring out the bus window. "Victory Patch Adorns Geraghty's Head," the caption read.

There were reports on others too. Pitcher Pete Barisoff, new to the Spokane team, had been treated for cuts and bruises and immediately released. Levi "Chief" McCormack was "doing nicely and is expected to be released from the hospital," and was reported to feel well enough to joke that his tomahawk could not have created a more perfect "V" on the top of Ben Geraghty's head (though it was Ben who had said it).

Gus Hallbourg also survived. The "right-handed pitcher is in the hospital [here] with a burned right hand but otherwise is in good condition and will be released soon."

There was news about who escaped the tragedy. "Milt Cadinha, Spokane's ace chucker, and Joe Faria, another right-hander, were not aboard the bus, the pair driving to Bremerton with their wives in Faria's car." Dutch Anderson was reported to have missed the bus ride due a personal matter that had taken him to San Francisco.

And then there was Jack Lohrke: "Jack Lohrke, outstanding young third baseman, was recalled by San Diego of the Pacific Coast League and fortunately was taken from the bus at Ellensburg and headed back to Spokane." This was one of the miracle stories – that just miles before the accident would take place, the highway patrol had tracked down the team and told them that Lohrke needed to head back to Spokane, as he had to report to San Diego in 24 hours. The call saved his life, people said to each other.

• • •

Survivors gathered in the halls of the Seattle hospital, where the beds were. There were too many wounded for everyone to get a room. Milt Cadinha and Joe Faria, the pitchers who had driven over with their wives, rushed to the hospital to be with their teammates. Families arrived; wives arrived. They wandered through the hallways, too. As did the souls who hadn't survived. Almost everyone collected there, in the corners of the hospital.

Ben could not let go of it – of how he had survived. Here he had come to Spokane to further his career. Had his sights on that manager job. Had even kept up hope that he would win it in the end, though he had become impressed with the leadership of Mel Cole, with that quiet but firm demeanor of his. And then this.

He would give anything for them all to come back to life again.

The souls continued to stay at the hospital, at least for the next day or so, partly because it was comforting to keep everyone together (alive or dead), partly because it was confusing to be anywhere else. Vic kept wandering from person to person, living or dead, whether they could hear him or not, saying, "I just need to get back to Spokane, to set everything up at the cabin," as though he were alive and just needed to take care of a few things before his family arrived in Spokane in July. Chris Hartje wandered with him, learning his story. The others floated between confused, quiet, angry, and sullen, with the occasional smile.

It wasn't that they stayed at the hospital all the time. Too many had too much to do. There was family to care for, all up and down the Pacific Coast.

But something, someone, kept drawing them back to a place where they could gather. And the hospital was that place, at least at first, since that was where their mates survived.

"Soon there will be a different spot in which to gather," the spirit-soul told Mel. "Back in Spokane. They'll need you there – all of them will need all of you," she said. "But then later, too, there will be a place to gather. Stay tied to them, Mel Cole," she told him. He didn't know why she said it, but he did what she said. In the end, it seemed like the right thing to do.

There was something comforting for the living players to be able to remain at the hospital together. Even some of those who were released thought of ways to stay on at least a few more hours, so they could sit together and try to figure out why they had survived and others had not.

Some of the souls sat with the survivors as they talked. They also wanted to know how it was that these men survived when they had not.

Which was a thought the survivors all had. "It can't be true," the they said often enough. Repeated to each other. Repeated in their heads. Or, "how could this have happened?" they would say, shaking their heads. The souls listened in, joined in on the discussion.

It would go like this: the survivors (one or the other of them) would go through the list of dead and talk about him (*he* was a good player ... *he* had a bad seat assignment on the ride over). Then they would go over the list of survivors and figure out how each had survived (*he* was up at the back of the bus, you know). Then they would take a break, only to start over again through the list, either out loud or in their heads.

In the midst of these periodic litanies, the souls would begin their own debate. Maybe it was because this person needed to keep playing (although that didn't explain the Kid's death). Or, maybe Jack got off the bus to save Gus (his seatmate).

"Maybe it's 'cause they had kids already," George Risk said at one point about the survivors. This created a roar – three pregnant wives, George? There were kids on the way for three of the dead – it couldn't be that! argued some of the other souls.

"Maybe it's because, if someone's got to die, it's better if it's a dad who doesn't know his kid yet," Risk persisted.

George Lyden shook his head no. "*I* got kids already – two boys – and look at all the good it did *me*," he said, gesturing with his spirit-hand at his dead form. Then he glared at Risk. "What're you saying, George? I died 'cause I'm a bad father?"

Mel stepped up. "Stop this," he said quietly, looking into the faces of the living men, especially Levi. He knew that Levi felt each of them whenever any of them were around. Ben, too, and the others a little, but Levi the most. "These men can feel you here. And *this* man can hear you. He's got a sense of you when you're around. You want him to hear you argue about whether *they* should be the dead ones?"

They hung their heads in shame then. "No, 'course not," George Lyden said. "Nobody shoulda died, is all. Sorry, Chief," he said to the strong tall man before him.

But Levi sensed what they had said and damned his survival in place of their own. They could tell in the way he walked, talked. Outwardly, he smiled. But it was the way he held his body that let them know.

And it wasn't just Levi. Nearly everyone questioned his own survival.

Ben was one who questioned it the most. "I was lucky," was what he said. "Shoulda been me," was what he thought. He wondered why he had been spared. Here he was, a brand new player to the team. He almost didn't come to Spokane at all. Shouldn't it be that he was brought here to die? Otherwise, why bring him here? Chris Hartje got here just in time to die, Ben thought ruefully about the catcher who he had just missed in Brooklyn, who had signed up with the Indians just nine days before crash.

And then there was his guilt. Ben could not stop thinking about how he had wanted to take over the manager's job from Mel, whose commitment to the team could not be questioned. Shouldn't *Ben* have been the one to die instead of Mel, as punishment for having such mutinous thoughts? Ben felt badly, too, that he had stolen Freddie's job at second. Then, it had been the luck of the draw. Now it just seemed wrong.

Others felt guilt too. For them, it was about what they didn't do. They didn't go back into the bus to save their mates. They didn't grab one of the ones in the seats nearby who had passed out. They didn't start praying soon enough.

The fewer his injuries, the worse each survivor felt. The crash couldn't have been so bad if all I did was burn my hand (or hurt my shoulder, or gash my head open)....

Never mind that the bus immolated as it rolled hundreds of feet down the steep slope. Never mind that it was a miracle that any man survived. Never mind that they did what they could. For they were men of the body. And they were men of the game. They were men of this season, 1946, and they were men of this team, the Spokane Indians, who never say never, coming back as they did so often in the ninth, in the last moments of the game. These were not the kind of men who could take what happened lightly. "Shoulda been me," is what they thought.

It was a way to salve the guilt. For after "should" comes "could." And with "could" comes a sense of fate, over which no one has control. And once there is a sense of fate, then there can be a sense of peace. Destiny had called. It just hadn't called on them. Not to die, anyway. Not this time.

Ben felt that kind of guilt. Sure he wondered what he could have done to save this life, or that one. But his guilt went deeper, beyond the physical to his own motives. He prayed to God about it in those days after the crash. But that did not salve his guilt.

He didn't share his feeling of guilt with anyone. He could scarcely share it with himself. Yet the thoughts were there. And every time he thought about it — any of it — the crash, the dead, his guilt — his head would ache. It didn't help that he had nearly been scalped, he told the Chief, who laughed and helped him forget, if just for a moment.

Still, even with the headaches, he couldn't let it go. What kind of God would spare the ones He spared, take the ones He took, and give no reason why? "Levi, these men dying," he blurted out once. "Why? And the rest of us still alive. Makes no sense."

I'll make it count, he thought then. Not for naught. As he thought it, he wondered about where the thought had come from. But there it was. "Not for naught."

As the news evolved, its minutiae grew. There was, for instance, an explanation that George Risk's body was taken to Kelso, Washington, as he really was from Cathlamet and not Hillsboro, Oregon, as listed in the roster. There was the exact time -6:25 a.m. – that George Lyden's mother and wife boarded their plane to fly to Seattle on June 25th to see their son and husband so close to death. No matter how small the fact, the newspaper assumed that everyone would want to know it, in the grand experiment of figuring out whether knowing "what" really could lead to knowing "why."

And even in all that "what," the "how" remained elusive. At first the "how" stayed elusive because the bus driver, Glen Berg, remained in such bad shape that he could not talk. The only available information was sketchy, though the paper reported it: "Officials said a gasoline station attendant at Vantage, Wash., told of an automobile in which passengers spoke of having sideswiped a bus. The attendant, however, was uncertain of the last digit in the license number, and the patrol was checking all licenses which might conform to his description." As it developed, and with so little information to go by, the search for the sideswiping car looked like it would go the way of the "why" – never to be found.

The paper's editorial staff also tried to capture what had happened by dedicating the first editorial on June 26th to the players – when the number of dead was not yet nine:

> The loss that the Spokane baseball club has suf-
> fered in the terrifying bus accident that sent eight

of the players to their deaths and critically injured and burned numerous others has stunned the entire community. Their tragic passing is universally mourned.

For these boys were fast earning the admiration and affection and team loyalty that baseball fans bestow upon earnest, enthusiastic, fair-dealing players of the hometown squad. Other players may later replace them on the team, but these fellows who met that horrifying death in the mountains will long be remembered and honored by local ball fans. And those who survive should not be forgotten as they lie in agony on hospital beds and slowly fight their way back to recovery.

In the annals of baseball there probably has been no equal to the tragedy that has befallen our team. But these keen-eyed youths who will play no more and those who will be away from the ball park for the coming months would without doubt want their fans to rally around as Spokane turns out again in force to echo the umpire as he resumes the game:

Play ball!

The writing seemed more a denial of grief than really an effort at grief itself. The near-cheerful tone at the end seemed to miss the enormity of the circumstance. And the editorial from The Spokane Chronicle – The Spokesman's sister newspaper in town – was a little better, remembering how they won their last game – by winning in the ninth:

THEIR LAST GAME IS FINISHED

A lightning-fast triple play, and it was all over.

Leave the park reverently, you who honor youth. It's all over, and what's the use to question the decision? The bases loaded and nobody down – and

then, one two three! Spokane's classy ball team hit
into a triple play they didn't have a chance to beat.

Last night's bus disaster in Snoqualmie pass will
be written in the impassive records as one of the
worst in all baseball history. Into the hearts of thousands of Spokane fans it will carry the crushing re-
alization that even the young and dauntless can not
always hit safely when the black sox team of fate is
in the field.

They were young; that's the pity of it; full of the
zest of living. No one could have guessed when they
laughed and jostled their way into that ill-starred
bus yesterday that they were through playing the
grand old game.

There is something of comfort in this! That in
their last game in Spokane they won, and with a
ninth-inning rally. Did you know, Bob James, when
you drove that last hit into center field, saving the
day, that it was the last play for you and your dough-
ty young teammates? But of course you didn't, for
the young always look forward to yet another game.

Stalwarts the like of whom flashed across the
Spokane field do not come into the world for naught.
Let us believe, with all the glorious young, that there
are other fields and other games ahead.

Mel heard the survivors talking about both columns and wondered. What *would* his men want? The re-start of the season? Grief
forever? Not grief forever. But who knew? In this moment, maybe
they would want that. And would those dead want something different from those still alive? He watched Dick Powers fighting to survive his broken neck. Mel knew he would make it. The living didn't
know it though. It was just one more way that there was chaos for
the living. And he knew full well that there was chaos for the dead.
There was just too much chaos for the living and the dead for him to
sense a consensus of what the men would want. Besides, he hadn't

yet asked what *he* wanted. He was too busy checking from man to man to think much about that.

Not all editors missed. There were editorial decisions that must have been meant to speak to the emotions. They re-ran, for instance, the text of the last game, which they had won. The story took on whole new meanings after the bus crash. "Spokane Fights Back" was one subheading that spoke, now, of the players who were fighting for their lives. "Spokane made its final bid a winning one" pulled an ache out of hearts all over town. "Levi McCormack was passed" – in the game, by the pitcher; in the fire, by fate.

And the subheading "Lohrke Afire" – thank God it had not been a foreshadowing of that player's fate. Yet the rest of that part of the story drew chills:

> Jack Lohrke, Spokane's sensational third base-man, continued his great play afield and contributed four hits in the evening contest, including a line drive 380 feet over the clock to the left of the scoreboard in left center field. The ball must have just barely missed putting the timepiece out of order.

The exaggeration of the quote now seemed ominous: why, of all days, had the reporter spoken of knocking out the timepiece? And what if, instead of missing, Jack actually *had* knocked the timepiece out? Was it his own clock that he left ticking – that stole him from the bus just before it crashed? Or had his intuition been trying to take out the clock for his mates, so that time could stand still and it would never turn June 24th?

Other eerie parallels felt deliberate. "NINE IN JEEP ESCAPE HURTS," one heading read (and ran right next to the most recent Spokane Indians update):

> The miracle, police reported, was not that none of the occupants of the former army jeep was seri-ously hurt when it turned over early today on Man-hattan (NY) bridge. The miracle was how nine per-sons squeezed themselves in the vehicle.... The jeep was borrowed from a friend by Arthur Witkowsky, who rounded up some friends and started for Co-ney Island. On Manhattan bridge the jeep skidded,

> struck the side structure and overturned. All nine occupants were thrown to the roadway. Later they were treated at Cumberland hospital for cuts and bruises and sent home. The jeep was wrecked.

It was impossible in reading the paper that morning not to imagine, at least fleetingly, how the nine dead Spokane Indians players might have helped to save the lives of these other nine. Did the Spokane players actually save them – did their souls cover the jeep like an umbrella? Or was it simply the loss of their nine lives that saved these others, as though God had decided not to take more lives of men who could survive war but not its aftermath? Either way, or in other ways, the questions came.

Another parallel: "INDIAN SERVICE OFFICES MOVED" ran right next to "CITY TO REPLACE PLAYERS' BLOOD." The article was just about the federal government. But the headline grabbed the attention of the subconscious, if nothing else. And how could it not? It was all the town could think about: their Spokane Indians.

And then there was the front page on June 27th: on either side of the article about Chris Hartje's death ran stories connected to Indians. To the left the headline read, "INDIAN BLANKET ON HART COFFIN." A different man, a different death – this one a California man, a "pioneer movie cowboy" no less – yet a headline just next to the column about Chris Hartje (another Hart) having died the night before. To the right the headline read: "NINE STARVING INDIANS RECEIVE FOOD FROM AIR," and told of nine Indians isolated by floods for three weeks, saved from starvation only "after a mercy flight by Russ Baker, veteran northern flyer" who "flew in supplies to the Indians at Thorn lake, 250 miles northwest of here, and dropped instructions to guide them to civilization." And so Christian Hartje was flanked. On one side of him, there was an Indian blanket draping a Hart coffin (for comfort, perhaps); on the other side, there were nine Indians whose lives were spared in a manna-from-heaven sort of way by a "mercy flight" and a military flyer. In the midst, too, a baby was born (on the island – it was why there were nine and not just eight Indians to save, the article said). Another parallel to lives lost and babies born, with three babies on the way, including for Chris. And there was a map dropped in amongst the food. Within the articles was all that any one could need – sustenance so that no one starves, a map so that no one loses the way, and a blanket to give comfort in the cold. They contained, too, what Chris would have sought for himself (in life, in death). Including the birth of a baby.

It was hard to tell if these parallel headlines and stories were purposeful. If they were, then they showed at least one newsman trying to speak to Spokane in ways beyond mere facts – trying to give readers more to imagine than what the naked sports articles' words gave them. If, on the other hand, they were just coincidences, then they were the kind of coincidences that is driven by synergy, by fate's own desire to have its story told in every way. Whether from conscious or subconscious endeavor, the headlines were evidence that at least one newsman could feel, respond to the path of fate. And what else was there to do in this aftermath but try to follow the currents? It was the only way to survive: moment by moment. In this moment, this. In that moment, that. What made things worse was knowing that there would be no second chance. They had been playing it down to the wire all season long, stealing the win in the waning moments of games that were otherwise lost. But how could they pull this one out? All last moments were gone. All that was left was the moment they were in.

There he was, still making the rounds, almost in a daze, any-more....

There was only two ways for Mel to stay focused. One was to listen to the spirit-soul. The other was to listen to Levi. The spirit-soul made sense. She looked like an angel almost, with her soft, pure light and lack of specific form. Levi, on the other hand – he had a lot to say to Mel. Mostly it was encouragement. Just as Mel spoke softly into the others, Levi spoke into Mel, in hushes and reassur-ances, with images of light. It was guidance, in a way, but guidance of a kind without form. It was as though Levi spoke in a foreign language that Mel had never heard. But it was a language calm and pure, and Mel could use all the help he could get, so he never said no to either of them.

The community tried, too, to put some semblance of order in the chaos that came after nine men had died.

At very first they did the first thing they could do. They replaced the blood that the dead and wounded had used up while in Seattle hospitals. It was a call to the community – provide blood for our blood.

Nearly as immediately, they formed a committee to organize a fund to raise money for the victims and families. Then there was talk of a fundraiser – a memorial game, backed by baseball. Articles ran every day about the committee's progress. Early on, one article spoke of how, in outlining the purposes and parameters of a fundraiser, the speaker broke down and wept. Other articles showed the community's efforts at financial support. "Citizens Backing Dependents' Fund," said one, written just two days after the crash. It told of how "several Spokane groups have started funds to aid the dependents of the nine dead Spokane baseball players." "Fans Eager To Aid Players' Families" came another, and told of how, when Bill Ulrich, former owner of the Indians, learned that Mel Cole's widow had put her Spokane home up for sale, "[he] offered $1,000 to be used in any way to help her and any of the others." And then there was Bing Crosby, a Spokane native, who contributed $1,000 to the fund, bought tickets for players' families for the memorial game, and got his buddy Bob Hope to contribute $500. They two had just been to Spokane for a golf tournament in early June....

And still, with all that activity, what does a man do when he comes home to his 8-year-old son who says why, and how, and say it's not true, Dad, say it's not true?

And they wrote. The community wrote. Some wrote in near-maudlin tones:

> Sports Editor, The Spokesman-Review: The following is entitled "The Better Land," and is by "Uncle Walt" Mason of the Emporia (Kan.) Gazette:

> "There is a better world, they say, where tears and woe are done away; there shining hosts in fields sublime, are playing baseball all the time, and there (where no one ever sins) the home team nearly always wins. Upon that bright and shining shore, we'll never need to sorrow more; no umpires on the field are slain, no games are called because of rain. So let us live that we may fly, on snowy pinions, when we die, to where the pitcher never falls, or gives a man first base on balls; where goose-eggs don't adorn the score and shortstops fumble nevermore."

> Jack C. Knight

Others wrote poignant pictures of how the sadness had hit every one:

> Sports Editor, The Spokesman-Review: Perhaps hard old timers in the service should not weep, and post exchange girls should be able to perform their work like they do every day. But such was not the case today out at Geiger field.
>
> For I saw tears in the eyes of soldiers, and the girls certainly were not themselves. Because there were a number of us here that saw the Spokane team in action this year and followed every move on foreign fields. We are dumbfounded out here. Every morning a group of us would discuss the last game played.
>
> The civilian gentleman I work for couldn't even come to the job today. And although a vet of 23 years, I am in a daze today. I pray to the Almighty to spare those so critically injured. And a prayer for those, and their families, that the Almighty God beckoned.
>
> M/Sgt. Conrad Rinehart

Still others wrote simply. The grief was too full to hold in:

> Sports Editor, The Spokesman-Review: With a heavy heart I send you these few lines. My husband and I are happy that we were able to attend the last game here and will always remember what a very good game it was. I know all the fans feel the same. The players are all loved, and will always be remembered.
>
> Mrs. E.L. White

• • •

Two boys sat in the grass next to the trickling creek. "Remember how they threw us that ball?" one said to the other, speaking of the day that Bob James and Bob Paterson had thrown them pop-ups to catch. "Sure," the other said, nodding. They drew their memory into the mud with sticks – you were standing there, I was over here, here was them....

It had been a moment they thought they would always remember. Now it became a moment they could never forget.

Three women collected in the Coles' kitchen. Just a week or so earlier, those three had gathered in the same spot. That time, their husbands – Mel Cole, George Risk, Bob Paterson – had been in the recreation room downstairs. This time they were not.

The women gathered for a purpose. Each was on her way home – away from Spokane. They were the three wives left. The three available. They hadn't gone to the hospital in Seattle. There had been no need. And now, even though they just wanted to go home, as in-laws prepared funerals, they couldn't leave. It felt wrong to just leave. So they gathered in that kitchen one more time.

"Let's start with 'thank you,'" Marjie said about the statement Mimi Cole would be making on their behalf. Mimi wrote that down: "Thank you for all you've done...."

It didn't sound right. "It's wrong," Mimi said, and scratched it out. She knew why, and started again. "We can never thank you enough," she said out loud, slowly as she wrote. The other two nodded. That was right. They couldn't. Even in the midst of their grief, they had been stunned by how grieved Spokane was as well. As though the town had tried to cry a portion of their tears.

They didn't feel the spirit-soul standing with them, looking over their shoulders. But they seemed to feel the whisper of her voice as she spoke into them as they wrote.

The efforts of the community did not go unnoticed. "PLAYERS' WIVES THANK SPOKANE: Mrs. Mel Cole Expresses Appreciation To Fans:"

> An expression of sincere appreciation to the citizens of Spokane for their kindness, cooperation and sympathy during the trying period which they are all going through, was made yesterday by Mrs. Mel Cole, wife of Spokane's baseball manager who

was killed in the bus tragedy in Snoqualmie pass last Monday night.

Speaking for the wives of two other deceased players, Mrs. George Risk and Mrs. Robert Paterson, Mrs. Cole said:

"We can never thank the wonderful people of Spokane enough for everything they have done for us since the terrible accident, but we do want every one to know we appreciate their kindnesses, courtesy and sympathy...."

Mrs. Risk returned to Hillsboro, Ore., and Mrs. Paterson flew to San Francisco prior to Mrs. Cole's departure, but urged her to convey their heartfelt thanks to the entire city of Spokane....

The paper reported that Mrs. Cole hadn't departed yet: "Her husband's military funeral was held in Sacramento" the day before she relayed her thanks, "but her doctor refused to permit Mrs. Cole to make the trip to California" because of the baby "due in September." Instead she left by car to Wenatchee, to be with her mother.

It was no way to say goodbye for her, Mel thought, as he stood by Mimi and sent thoughts of comfort, best he could. It was just too much for her. That was a part he regretted – how it made her feel. How it all made her feel.

"That's right, Kid. We lived right near each other," Chris said.

It was all that seemed to calm Vic – a recitation of that last talk that he and Chris had had as they rode on the bus from Spokane.

"And we went to the same ball game back home?" Vic asked again, to remember.

"Yes, we did," Chris said, and relived the game with him one more time.

Mel stepped up. "How's he doing, Chris?" he asked the veteran catcher.

Chris nodded at Vic, shrugged at Mel. "Best as can be expected," he said.

They all knew now what Vic had been "sick" about – how the combination of his career stalling that summer and his family being without him had been almost more than he could bear. How he had been holding on to his family's arrival in Spokane in July as his saving grace. And now this.

"I'm going home now," Vic said.

Chris shook his head. "No, son. Not this time. Not like you think." His own heart ached at the truth of the words. It took all that he had not to break down himself.

"He needs you," Mel said, and Chris held himself together, nodding. Bob Paterson looked up to see if Chris needed help, but Chris waved him off. This time, Chris would help Vic by himself.

"But I would like to go home," Vic said. "You said it yourself – if you miss your family, go home! You said that, Chris," Vic said, almost accusingly, remembering Chris' words from the bus ride. "Besides, I told you – Betty and I – we're taking Bobby to the park this afternoon," Vic said. "Or maybe – am I supposed to go back to Spokane to set up the cabin?" he asked, but with less enthusiasm, as though he were vaguely remembering that things had changed but could not remember why, or how. "No, it's back home that I need to go," he said, trying to remember. "Season's over. We're getting ready for the wedding...." He trailed off and looked at Chris for confirmation.

Chris shrugged, and shook his head no. "Things have changed," Chris said.

"Can I at least go see my family?" Vic asked quietly.

"Sure," Chris said, and he whisked the Kid off to San Francisco yet another time to look in on Vic's grieving family, and to try to help Vic remember what had happened.

In the midst of it all, the bus driver recovered enough so that he could speak. His recollection "left little doubt there was a passenger car involved in the accident," the paper reported.

> Berg reported to patrolmen trouble with bus brakes and engine and told how he had met a car on the wrong side of the road before the accident. He stepped on the gas to have a better chance to get by, the injured driver said.

Berg told Coroner John P. Brill the accident, which has cost nine lives, was caused by the other automobile, which forced the bus off the highway.

Berg said the bus had brake and engine trouble en route to Seattle from Spokane and stopped at Ellensburg for repairs, "which didn't seem to do any good."

He said that just before the accident he exchanged headlight blinks with a passing truck, the truck's signal indicating the road ahead was clear. However, Berg said, he met an automobile coming on the wrong side of the road a moment later.

Berg said he did not apply the brakes "because I was afraid this would make the bus skid and throw us into the guard rail. I stepped on the gas to 'goose' it so we would have a better chance of getting by."

"It seemed like the car hit us as I felt a jar at the left, front and end," Berg continued. "We then struck the guard rail and began taking out the posts, one by one, and I lost control." He estimated his speed at the time as about 28 miles per hour.

The state patrol continued its search for the mystery car.

More facts, written nearly in a circular fashion, capturing every word the man said, repetition be damned. The words did give a little more information about what. They failed to give any more insight, though, into why – at least not why from God's eyes.

The dead lacked that insight too. Why, God, why? they said, and grumbled amongst themselves. It was wrong, what had happened. A mistake. A thief in the night had taken their lives, and they were not going to take it, they said, as they threatened a rebellion they had never felt when they'd been alive. They weren't going on to somewhere else, some said, arms crossed, rooted in between life and death, determined to stay right where they were. Others, like

Freddie and Vic, drifted away. Mel tried to call them back, as the spirit-soul urged. But he could feel them drifting away. George Risk was one, too – sometimes Mel had to ask George to come forward so many times that he wondered if George could hear him – and then he would see his soul come through the hospital hall, where he had gone to look for him. George Lyden, too, seemed anxious to be gone.

And they were getting tired of him fussing at them.

But the spirit-soul would not let up. "Help them," she said yet again.

Mel looked at her, distressed. "What can I do?" he said. "Can I tell them they're wrong? That it *wasn't* a thief that stole their lives? That they survived the war just to die? I can't say those words. Not and mean them, too."

She looked at him with a steady gaze. "Do you believe all that?" she asked.

Mel looked away. Thought of God, in whom he still believed. Thought of Levi, who seemed to see beyond what Mel knew. "No," Mel said. "It can't be that."

She nodded, and waved her hand in the direction of the dead. "Look at them," she said. "What do you see?"

He looked. "What do you mean?" he finally said.

"Their light," she said.

And then he saw what she meant. The ones who wandered off the most were the ones whose light had begun to dim. It was as though their disconnection from Mel and the team, and any sense of hope, was somehow also disconnecting them from this glow of light they had all become after they had died. And while he was new at death, Mel knew how, the closer he was to a true thought, the brighter he felt, and knew he looked. It was the same with the others. Bob Kinnaman couldn't have glowed much brighter as he stood watch over George Lyden's bed that first night, as George died. And Chris – for as reluctant as he had been to die, his light was strong as he connected to Vic. The more he worked to keep Vic connected to him, the stronger his light was.

And Mel knew the spirit-soul stayed brightest of all. Consistently bright, as though she came from a place where there were no doubts.

"She's right," he thought. "I need to stay tied to them."

"Remember that first night," she said, sending him an image of creating a sense of safety. So that was what he tried. He tried to make things safe.

For awhile, that worked. But there came a time when he saw that there was no end to the chaos. And then he could take no more.

The chaos of that first night had made sense. It was the kind of chaos that creates order. The chaos of the next night – that too made sense. It was aftermath chaos, the sense of what to do now that the immediate crisis has ended.

This chaos, though, was beyond aftermath. It was never-ending. And Mel did not want to be in it anymore.

And so it was that, on the day after Mimi left with her mother to go live in Wenatchee while she waited for their child to be born, he lost his tolerance for death.

I think it was watching the movers that caused him to fall apart. It was as though each thing they took from the house took away one more piece of his dream (for as dead as he now was) to build a haven for his players. Suddenly, Mel couldn't stand it. The others were right. Why bother to survive the war – put off the very living of their lives – if all would be for naught? Where was the point in that?

He rushed from mover to mover. "Stop it! Stop! We're not moving. I'm not going to die," he said, getting louder and louder as each word left his mouth (and as everything around him got darker and darker, like a thundercloud was overhead).

Then he stopped, struck by the futility of it, of yelling into an impervious face. He sat on the stoop, head in his hands, as the movers, oblivious to his rant, walked through him as they carried boxes from the home to the truck. Let them walk through me, he thought, as they loaded up the last of it. What does it matter.

"Hello," he heard.

Mel looked up. A little boy stood in front of him. "Are you okay?" the little boy asked. Mel shook his head no, slowly though.

"Can you see me?" he asked the boy. Is this a dream? he thought to himself – wondered, if it was, which part was the dream.

The boy shook his head yes. "I can see you," he said. "I'm a part of you." He smiled. "I'm your son."

Mel sat in disbelief.

"Not yet, of course. I'm still to be born."

Mel believed him then. He saw in him his eyes. His wife's hair. He was a beautiful child. No child had ever been more beautiful than this child before him.

"I know you feel bad," the child said, "about leaving me. And my mom. Me, too," he said, a little wistfully. "I'm sad you're leaving, too. After I'm born, and as I grow up, I'll even be mad about it.

"But there's this time now," he went on. "When I'm a soul to be born and you're a soul that's just died. Between us, we can talk right now."

The boy looked around at the yard. "You were going to plant some trees right over there," he said, pointing to the edge of the yard.

"After the season," Mel said, nodding. "For shade. At the edge. And on the day you were born, I was going to plant one right in front, for you." Mel sighed. "I'm so sorry I'm dead," he said.

The boy nodded. "I kinda have known. Just a sense, and not for sure, but it was almost already done, you know, even before I came along."

The boy sat on the stoop next to Mel. He picked up Mel's spirit hand and held it in his own.

"You used to take this hand to feel me kick – even just a week ago," he said. "And you stood in the backyard too, and thought of the two of us playing ball together – boy or girl, you were going to teach me how to throw," he said, laughing.

Mel smiled. "You sure do know a lot already."

The boy nodded, pleased that his father seemed happy to see him. His face changed to a more serious look.

"I know you'll always love me," the boy said. "And I know you'll watch over me – not on Earth, not on the ground, or where I'll hear you tell me what to do or how to behave, or to mind my mother, or things like that. But you'll see me grow up, and you'll be right there any time I need you. And maybe I won't know that, once I'm born and start to live. Maybe I'll never know that all I have to do is imagine you right beside me for you to be there. But I know it now," the boy said. "I know now you will always be there, if I ever ask. Or even if I don't ask. And I know now that you always loved me." He nodded slowly. "And I know now that, even if you died, you died while you were doing what you loved to do." He smiled. "I promise I'll try to learn to throw."

Mel hugged his son, tousled his hair, kissed his temple, and felt the dark cloud drift away. "I would give anything to have stayed alive," he said. The boy nodded. And was gone as suddenly as he had appeared.

• • •

Mel walked through the hospital halls, looking for Chris. As though hearing his name, Chris appeared, Vic in tow.

"I have something to tell you, Chris – Freddie too," Mel said. He called over Bob James, who brought Freddie with him. Bob sat with Vic so that Chris could sit with Mel and Freddie.

Mel told them then of his son, and of seeing his son. He told it all to them – of his anger, and then calm, and then the boy. "Maybe you can see your child too," he said when he was done, to these two men whose wives were pregnant. "It's something to try."

Chris nodded. Freddie's face looked blank, as though the English was beyond him. "My niño," Mel said, using the Spanish word for child. Freddie nodded then, but still sat still.

Mel thought about what more he could say to help Freddie understand. Then he realized that it wasn't that Freddie didn't understand him. It was that Freddie was trying to stand still so that the baby could find him. It was how Mel's boy had found Mel – in one of those moments where everything is still.

Mel nodded. "I think that's right," he said to Freddie. "Correcto," he said, and Freddie couldn't help but grin at Mel's very bad Spanish.

"I tell you if I meet my child – te diré," Freddie said.

"Me, too," Chris said. Paused. Waited. Looked into the air, as if looking into the moment he was in. And then he grinned. "Our baby's a girl!" he said.

Baseball grieved, too, and did what organizations do – it moved away from grief into action.

The team itself – the Spokane Indians, by and through its owner and front office – at first just stood like deer in headlights. That was all they could do. "Sam Collins was nearly prostrate last night when The Spokesman-Review notified him of the accident," the newspaper explained. And while the league wanted to know what would happen, "naturally both Collins and Dwight Aden, business manager of the club, were too shocked to think of more than the serious business immediately ahead of them."

The prediction was right – Sam and Dwight had immediate concerns about young men, both dying and dead, that kept them from thoughts of baseball:

> Admittedly "up in the air and terribly tired," Sam
> W. Collins continued to carry on under the ever-in-

creasing burden of grief and worry as news continued to come in concerning the tragic bus accident.
With less than three hours' sleep in 48 hours, Collins
was back in the team's offices taking care of the details at this end while Dwight Aden, business manager, and Ken Hunter, publicity director, are in Seattle
taking care of the injured players' wants, arranging
for rooms for the relatives of the players and many
other important details.

The paper spoke of how, in spite of ill health, Sam worked non-
stop arranging for families' transportation, sending his own daughter to travel with Ben Geraghty's wife, sending Bob Paterson's wife
home to San Francisco, ensuring that the Geraghtys' three children,
"Patrick, 6 ½, Mary Elizabeth, 5, and Barry, 18 months, were taken
care of...."

And so on.

The team's immediate concerns left little energy for reflection on
what to do with the rest of the season. The league, however, would
not hear of a time gap, no matter how Dwight Aden objected (said
the newspaper), no matter how Dwight explained that "Owner Sam
Collins' health is such that such a meeting should be postponed."

And so it was that the meeting was held and the decision was
made: the Indians would begin playing again no later than July
4th.

It had taken three days for nine to die. It would take 11 days to
replace them.

Perhaps such quick movement in deciding the Indians' rest-of-
the-season future was the only way, since it allowed the nation's
baseball culture a way to move. Even before a start-up time was
designated – even before they knew if there would be a start-up
time – baseball was reaching out to help. The president of the National Association of Minor Leagues offered to assist in any way.
The team from Stockton, California – a rival in preseason play – also
offered any and all assistance. The president of the Pacific Coast
League urged every team in that league to send surplus players to
Spokane. Branch Rickey, general manager of the Brooklyn Dodgers
and well known for his expansive farm team system, also wired his
assistance. "Just heard report of terrible disaster to your club. Will
make every possible effort to send players to you if you need coop-
eration," he said within a day of the crash. He sent another telegram

offering to assist Sam in finding a "topnotch manager" for the rest of the season.

Privately, Dwight disagreed. Getting back to baseball at the same time as taking care of all the rest? What about Ecclesiastes? To everything there is a season, and a time to every purpose under heaven. This was not time to play ball. There were other verses: a time to live, a time to die; a time to weep and a time to laugh; a time to mourn, and a time to dance; a time to cast away stones, and a time to gather them up.... Dwight never did take out his Bible and read those verses from start to finish. There was no time. Besides, in the end, it was what Sam wanted – to keep the game moving. It was his way. So Dwight kept on moving on every front.

Regionally too, teams did what they could. The fundraiser became their beacon for effort. It wasn't clear how it came up – had Spokane asked them to play in a memorial game or had the leagues suggested it on their own?

Either way, by the June 28th paper, just days after the crash, everything was set:

> The Western International and Pacific Coast baseball leagues announced their intentions yesterday of putting on the biggest benefit baseball night in the west's history of the sport as proceeds from four games the night of July 8 will be turned over to the wives and parents of the dead and injured Spokane baseball players.
>
> On that night two Pacific Cost league teams, the Oakland Acorns and the Seattle Rainiers, will play at Ferris field in an exhibition and at the same time exhibitions will be played in three Western International league parks. Victoria will play at Tacoma, Yakima at Bremerton and Salem at Vancouver. Proceeds from all games will be turned over to the fund.... Whole-hearted cooperation has been pledged by the cities' various sports writers, players, owners and citizens.

And local amateur teams did what they could to help. Everywhere the eye traveled, there were spontaneous fundraisers raising money for the fund in bits and pieces. Nearly every day, an article appeared in the newspaper, expounding on yet another effort by yet another group. Even the prison team down in Walla Walla, known for its good play, was going to be allowed to play "outside" in a benefit game.

In the midst of the trauma, in the midst of the promise to remember, the headlines started to focus on a re-start of the season. "SHATTERED TEAM TO PLAY AGAIN: Collins And Abel Conferring: Will Rebuild Indians." "SPOKANE INDIANS HOLD INITIAL WORKOUT AS REBUILDING BEGINS: Additional Aid Expected To Arrive Soon." "REBUILT INDIANS TO PLAY JULY 4: Resume Schedule With Six Game Series With Yakima."

Mel went from soul to soul. "Ferris Field," he told them each. "We'll meet at the baseball field." He had begun to learn how to call them together. Time, date, place were less important than the sense he would send to each and every one. It was something he had learned how to do from the spirit-soul. Levi, too, had taught him. He couldn't say how, but it was true. Levi knew things that Mel did not know how he knew.

Each of the Bobs was so clear that Mel hardly had to call them to him. Others, though – George Risk, the Kid – their chaos was stronger, so he was constantly out in search of them. "Ferris Field," he would say to remind them. He relied on the others, too, to help out those most lost in the chaos.

It helped to have events on the horizon. There was the first day of practice, with new players coming all across the country to try out. There was the first day of the season beginning again – July 4th (another birth day). And there was the memorial game, set for July 8th. It was just around the corner.

It helped, too, to have contact with the children yet to be born. Word had spread that he, Freddie and Chris had talked to their children's souls. The other souls gathered to hear the details. And while each child's spirit had had special words just for each one of the fathers-to-be, there was something in those words for all the players. The words of the children created pathways to the core of these men's existence, and helped keep them grounded to the moment.

And then Freddie brought it all together. At first his spirit was so excited about the soul of his child that he nearly missed the look on Bob James' face. Then he realized: this was not something that Bob could have. No wife, no child. It was not there for him.

"Mi amigo," Freddie said. "My friend. You are like my brother. If we live, you love my child. But we die." He searched for words, but could not find the English. "Me ayudas, no? Help me? En la vida, en la muerta, esta niña necesita ambos nosotros – todos," he said, waving his hand at every soul. "The child – for everyone," he said. "My team. Help me, no?"

"I get it, Freddie," Chris said. "I know what you're saying." He turned to the others. "Freddie, Mel and me – we may be their dads, but we're going to need help," he said. "So maybe – it's asking a lot, but maybe you all would be there for them? You know, in case we're not enough," he said. "Like – like god-uncles. But really from God."

"My kids, too," George Lyden said, thinking of his two young boys without a father now. "I'd sure appreciate the help," he said. He looked at George Risk in particular, the one who had said that maybe they had died because they didn't have children yet.

George Risk nodded. "Thank you," he mouthed to Lyden.

All the men nodded then, and made a pact. The children would have more fathers than ever imagined.

In that moment, Vic came forward. He had been listening closely. "Me too," he said. All the dead men looked at him. "For Bobby," he said, nodding slowly. "My sister, too, but Bobby – he's just a kid, you know? Just four. Like George's boys. I'll need help to help him."

They all stood quietly, looking at him. Vic nodded again. "I do know what I'm saying," he said. "I do know I've died. I do know I can't go home. Not alive." He looked from one to the other. "Will you help me?" They gathered around him then in support as if his knees gave way to the exhaustion of finally knowing the truth.

Dwight and Sam already had discussed it. Ben Geraghty was the perfect choice for manager. And Ben – he was all for it. Kept talking about how they would make a great comeback for those who had died. "We'll win this pennant yet," he said.

What none of the living knew, not even Levi – not yet – was that Ben already had made a promise to the dead that he would not let them die in vain. That he would, somehow, make what happened count.

• • •

In the third day of reports about the crash, The Spokesman speculated that "Ben Geraghty, second baseman, who was one of the less seriously injured of the team members, might manage the rebuilt club. 'He won't be able to play for some time, of course, but he can manage,'" the paper said, quoting the owner.

Then the June 28th paper reported that it was official:

Dwight Aden, club business manager, and Joyce Collins, club secretary, said tonight that Ben Geraghty "definitely" had been selected to manage the decimated Spokane baseball club. Geraghty came out of the tragic bus crash in Snoqualmie pass Tuesday with a scalp wound and a broken knee cap.

Late today he conferred by telephone with President Sam Collins ... and said he hoped to get an early start after arrival in Spokane tomorrow at approximately 7 a.m., to map plans for reorganization of the club which numbered nine killed and six injured.

Ben and Levi boarded the plane. They were on their way back to Spokane. Ben could not stop talking. Levi knew how to listen. Ben was lucky to have him there.

As they settled in, Ben decided it was time. "I've made a promise," he said to Levi, "to the men who died. 'Not for naught,' is what I said."

Levi nodded. "It's what I've said too."

This, then, was their bond.

"Tell me everything," Ben said. So Levi did. He spoke of each of the Bobs, the Georges and the Kid. He spoke of Mel and Freddie – both quiet men of steel reserve. Much like Levi, Ben thought – at least, the steel reserve part – and he wondered at what fate would bring him to the three of them – Freddie's job at second, Mel's job as manager, and Levi himself as Ben's right hand, guiding Ben through all of what he would learn, as he took on the job that he had come to conquer.

The June 30th Spokesman showed Ben Geraghty "going over reorganization plans" (with his "V for victory" scalp bandage). The July 2nd paper spoke of his management of the workouts, which he conducted on crutches.

And then the July 3rd paper reported that it was not going to work. Geraghty had been "benched by his physician."

"Taking over until Geraghty is able to work again was Glenn Wright, former Indians' manager, who resigned on the eve of the current season due to ill health," the paper reported. Wright did look like a solid choice, given his experience with the team earlier and his efforts to help the team now. "Wright has been performing double duty behind the scenes during the days since the accident, helping in many capacities at the club's office while Mrs. Wright took over the care of Geraghty children and helped in numerous ways to relieve the wives and families of the players," the newspaper reported. Spokane fans had wondered why Ben had been picked over Glenn Wright in the first place. Whatever the case, it was time to set aside differences. And so amidst the swirl of chaos that surrounded putting together a team in an 11-day turnaround, a leader – whether temporary, permanent, or in-between – had finally surfaced.

Added to the chaos of settling on a manager was the chaos of organizing a team. For it would be all brand new. "The only familiar Spokane players were Milt Cadinha and Joe Faria, pitchers who escaped the accident by driving in a car to Bremerton...."

Players surfaced from all over the country. By the last day of June, the Indians held their first practice:

> 11 players ... were on hand at Ferris for the initial practice since the tragic bus accident last Monday.... Sam Collins received offers of aid from teams throughout the nation.

> Those on hand for the first practice included Bill Smith, young Lake City (Iowa) infielder who told Collins, "I figured you might be needing some ball players, so I hitch-hiked out." He just received his Navy discharge but played considerable baseball in Hawaii.

The Spokesman bravely quoted names and statistics of the new players. Charley Bates was a "veteran first-sacker" who had "played 35 games with Oakland last year before being injured and had a .306 average;" Don Miles was a pitcher from the Portland Beavers with three years pro experience; Fred Pollett was an outfielder and pitcher with Salem before the war and had been in semi-pro ball in

Seattle in the current season; Mel Steiner was in from the Mexican League, where the food had not set well; the "one catcher" – Jerry Varrelman – "although small, impressed the Indian management."

The survivors who could make it to the field shook their heads at the ragtag team. "This'll never work," Milt Cadinha said to Joe Faria, the two pitchers who had avoided the bus crash by driving over to Seattle separately.

Trainer Dutch Anderson walked up. "It won't be so bad," he said hopefully, trying to convince himself more than them.

Milt sighed. "I wish we could just call it quits," he said. "You know – for the rest of the season. It doesn't seem right, to be here without them." Everyone nodded.

"Too bad Ben couldn't take over like they had planned," Dutch said. They all nodded again. Too bad, they said again, though they knew that Glenn Wright was looking better than he did at the start of the season, and seemed back on track.

Too bad, came an echo from a circle of souls that surrounded where the living players stood. They stood in the midst of the heart-ache of their mates and watched from afar the ones who had come to replace them.

And here was the question: wasn't Milt right? Hadn't this season been lost to the fire?

Mel stepped up. It seemed like he was always stepping up. He stood in front of all his men, both living and dead.

"This is what I can tell you," he said. "It may be that the season is lost. It may be that this team will not win another game. Not even one.

"But we didn't come to this field back when the season began to quit before we started. And we're not going to quit now.

"There is one thing I know, and if I know nothing else, I will always know this. This team – you men – you know how to do two things. You know how to be a team. And you know how to win.

"So this is what we give any man who enters this field, from now until eternity. We give them the desire to win. And we give them a mate."

He sat back down. His dead mates softly clapped. His living mates shielded their eyes from the bright, bright sun that had just made its way out from behind a cloud.

"Bob?" Bob Kinnaman heard a voice he recognized, though not as a sound. As a thought-sound. He turned around and saw the light form of an older man standing there.

"Dad?" Bob said. The older man nodded. "You've died," Bob said. His father nodded again. "Oh no. Poor mom. And sis. They can't lose us both in a week."

His father looked down. "You're right. But I've been sick long enough," he said – which was true, he had been sick for a long time. "And you needed me, son. I could tell. You needed me here. So this is where I needed to be."

In a flash, Bob remembered that first night with George Lyden, as Bob sat by George's side and helped him die, how he had known that his parents (had they known) would have wanted him to stay with George. He flashed on the agonies of the entire past week, of trying to stay strong and help Mel help the others, of not allowing himself to relax for fear of giving in to the chaos of emotions, of senses. He looked at his father and nodded. "I've really needed you," he said. If he had had eyes, he would have cried. He reached his father in a step.

On July 1, 1946, the Kinnaman family could hardly believe that they had to start preparing for a second funeral.

Ben was on the edge of despondent as he and his family readied to leave. They wouldn't be staying through the summer, he told Levi. "Sure wish we could stay," he said sadly. "But the doc won't let me even stand on the sidelines with my head the way it is. And health." He coughed. "I gotta recoup, if I'm coming back next season."

Levi nodded.

"Think you'll be playing?" Ben asked.

Levi looked away into the distance. He knew he hurt more than he would say. But he didn't want his season to be over either. Not if the team was starting back up. He chose his words carefully. "I know I want to," he said. "Like you said. For them."

Levi stood and looked in the mirror. And wondered why he had lived.

The chaos started settling down as the players started settling in. "Spokane's bereaved baseball fans are going to see their club in

action again Thursday," the paper was able to report on July 2nd.
"It won't be the same team that Spokane was watching battle its
way toward the top of the Western International League," the paper
warned, "but the Indians will be back in Ferris field, doing business
at the same old stand."

> Even at the last minute, though, it was chaos:
> With the Spokane Indians' first ball game since
> the team's tragic accident on Snoqualmie pass a bare
> 24 hours away, players from all over were signing in
> to the club's offices in the Empire State building so
> fast yesterday officials had a hard time keeping up
> with the flow.

The team was able to report the starting line-ups, although just
barely:

> An original member of the ill-fated team will be
> Milt Cadinha, a leading pitcher in the Western Inter-
> national league, going to the mound for the Indians.

> Drawing the backstop duties will be Jerry Varrel-
> man, former Lewiston player, recently with the Mex-
> ican league; or John Carroll, army dischargee.

> Other infield posts will be handled thus: Charley
> Bates, formerly of Oakland, first base; Lou Kubiak,
> on loan from Salem, shortstop; Mickey Wintraub, on
> option from Sacramento, second base; [Don] Ryan,
> third base.

> Drawing outfield jobs will be Frankie Hawkins,
> formerly of Oakland; Mel Steiner, recently out of the
> Mexican league, and Gale Bishop, former Washing-
> ton State college baseball and basketball star, pro-
> viding he reports before game time.

> Joe Faria will be the only original Indian on the
> team for the second game. He is slated to start on
> the mound in the seven-inning nightcap.

Milt Cadinha and Joe Faria were the only ones that the fans really knew. What an odd feeling it was – to read that list and know all the names that did not appear.

I think it was because he felt he had to do something. Maybe it was because he felt that, without doing something more, the nine who were dead could end up lost. And maybe he was right – maybe they could.

And I think he went where he went instead of somewhere else because he knew that, to do something, he needed help, more help than just normal ground could give. So he went where the river could help – this river that had a magic to it, that knew how to collect souls, just as it had, for centuries, collected tribes at the end of every harvest for celebration and trade, dancing and community, in the place where the waterfall is. Or maybe he went there because it was the place he knew. It was the place where he learned to love baseball. Maybe it was that simple, why he went there and not some other place. It was sometimes hard for me to tell with Levi why he did what he did. Though he did always seem to know best, in the end.

For whatever reason, late one night, it was as I had predicted: Levi the "Chief" McCormack had found his way back out to the land that used to be a ballfield out at Old Nat Park, out on the edge of town, with the river rushing beneath it. He came with a promise to keep and sweetgrass to burn. The promise was to remember. The sweetgrass was to help the dead souls heal.

He stood on the land, now a parking lot. He looked to the river, and to the sloping bank across the way where the military base was. He called out in his mind for Mel Cole, that young leader in life, young leader in death. Mel heard him and called for the others. In this way, in a little more than an instant, they were all there: a man and his nine dead friends.

What they shared belongs to them. But it seemed to me that Levi shared a lot – about death, about grief to overcome, about letting go of this world and staying in the next.... Words could not convey all of what he wanted them to know, but senses could, so he felt what he was sharing and they heard him through his senses. It seemed to me, as I watched the reunion, that Levi knew more about dying, and about how a soul stays connected to those he loves without losing his way, than any of the rest of us could know combined. In the end, whatever it was that he knew, thought, saw, felt – they did too.

Then Levi reached into his bag and pulled out a bat and ball. He flipped the ball into the air and hit it with the bat in just such a way that it sailed out of the lot and into the river. He stood and watched the current carry the ball until it bobbed out of sight.

Then he reached into his bag, pulled out another ball, and repeated what he had just done. And stood still as he watched the current carry the ball down the river and out of sight. Then he pulled out another ball and did the same thing again, watching until the ball was gone. And then he pulled out another ball and did the same thing again. And then another ball. And then another. And another. And another. And another. His eyes welled with tears as he watched each ball disappear down the river.

When all nine balls were gone, he rested two fingers from each hand on his cheeks where the tears were and then streaked the fingers across his cheeks. Then he dropped to the ground, and put his head in his hands. He could do no more.

Nine souls stood in front of Levi, between riverbanks, as if they were forming a bridge between boys hanging from the left field fence and military men standing on the opposite bank, all watching Babe Ruth hit a homerun in 1924. Nine souls stood as a bridge in front of Levi and watched what he did. And then they agreed. He was right.

The mutiny among the dead had subsided. All seemed ready for the inevitable. Staying would not be an option. Not on Earth. Not in a permanent way. Mel didn't even have to say it anymore. Everyone already knew. But staying, just now, *was* the right thing. After all, there were events to attend. The season re-opened tomorrow. The memorial game was five days away. Besides, it wasn't quite time yet to leave.

The chaos of the last minutes was too much; the win went to it.

July 5, 1946: "REVAMPED SPOKANE INDIANS LOSE PAIR TO YAKIMA"

The first sentence of the article said it all: "The Spokane Indians returned to the baseball wars yesterday afternoon and before the two games were completed the new players must have felt as if they had been through another war, too."

The article spoke of how four Tribe pitchers had to "go to the mound" in the first game; how the Spokane batters were not able to "connect solidly;" how the umpires made matters worse with their "alleged" umpiring; how they tossed both managers out of the game, fined a hotheaded player, and then fined pitcher Joe Faria "for asking them a question as they were on their way to the dressing room." "They seemed so consistently wrong that both teams were continually arguing and the crowd entered into the uprising with gusto. There was no apparent favoritism, both teams took a beating."

The newspaper evaluated, too, Spokane's chances to succeed during the rest of the season. It did not look promising. "Team Needs Time" was the subheading:

> Manager Glenn Wright fielded a team practically unknown to Spokane fans and it will take all of his skill to create a winner from the material he has on hand. Too many of them have been playing just occasionally during the season and will need quite awhile to get into the kind of shape it takes to play every day.

The newspaper talked about how Dutch Anderson had suddenly found himself back playing the sport that he thought he had finished. He wasn't even listed in the starting line-up from the day before, and there was no real explanation in the newspaper for how the decision to play him had come about:

> Few of the fans realized Anderson has been the Indian's trainer for the season and missed the fatal bus accident by flying to his home in California to take care of some personal business.
>
> He has a tough spot to fill, taking the place of hustling John Lohrke now playing regularly with San Diego, but Anderson is trying and that is all the fans ask.

Wins were not on the horizon either as the Indians lost the next two, and geared up for another double-header on July 7th. It was now 14 days since the crash, 12 days since the last of the nine had died, no days since they knew whether all remaining injured would survive or not, and no days since any of the bus riders had been able to play.

Then they lost their fifth game – the first in the double-header – 24 to 1. Unbelievable, to lose so badly. It doesn't even matter how, when the loss is so bad.

How badly must we play here? Milt Cadinha thought. He thought of Mel Cole, that young manager who had started his job on the eve of play, and of how Mel had made Milt the starting pitcher on opening night, way back on April 26th. Milt thought of the rest of his teammates from the team before the bus crash – how they had been able to read each other, like no other team he had ever known. Just to die? For what? He didn't know.

He only knew that, if he played, he would play for them.

Headline: Monday, July 8, 1946: SPOKANE SNAPS 5-GAME
   STREAK
Subheadline: Rebound After Losing Afternoon Tilt, 24 to 1

Milt Cadinha, Spokane's ace right-hander, last night shut out the Yakima Stars by pitching a masterful two-hit ball game, as his mates backed him up to win 12 to 0.

Determined to put the Indians back in the running, Cadinha pitched his heart with every throw.... His efforts led his mates to play what amounted to sparkling ball as the Indians won their first game in six starts since the tragic accident which decimated the team....

The whole team came to life in the night game to help Cadinha win his ninth game of the season... his first since the tragic accident.... From his first pitch the 1,265 paying customers could tell the big right-hander was out to win.

At the end of the season, the Indians were in seventh place, losing 52 of their final 74 games. Here they had been, a leader midway through a highly competitive and exciting year of baseball – and in one fell swoop, they plummeted to the bottom.

The salvageable part of the season was Glenn Wright's career. What had happened on the eve of opening night – the drinking binge – was something he worked to stop for the rest of his career. It was almost worth all the rest of the season's losses to see him figure out how to regain his way. The unsalvageable part though, even amongst the losses, was the orneriness of the team itself – their rough-and-tumble, fight-picking sorts of ways. Once they were mad at the bat boy because he didn't start a fist fight with the other team's bat boy during an all-out brawl they had started with the other team.

But on July 7th, no one knew that this riotous plummeting would be the way of the season – not for sure. True, things were not looking good. But who could tell? And so, before they knew for sure what a disastrous rest-of-season it would be, they were gifted this game. From God?

On that night of July 7th (14 days after the accident, 12 days after the last of the ninth had died, and one day before the memorial game), everyone knew who Milt Cadinha was pitching for. Everyone knew that he could pitch it no other way. Everyone knew who had helped him get that win – his ninth. Everyone knew who had helped him play – who had helped him "pitch his heart with every throw." And everyone knew that it had been through his play that "the whole team had come to life" one more time.

And then it was July 8th – the day of the fundraiser.

The goal was to raise $50,000, less than half of which could come from ticket sales. "We are not interested in just selling tickets to a ball game," one of the committee members said. "We are out to raise money to help the injured players and the families of those killed. The ball game will be well worth attending, but the primary interest of the people of Spokane must be to do the right thing by our ball club and its players."

The community did not disappoint. Contributions came as waves do – billows here, ripples there, but always consistently welling into a swell in the moment that the water hits the rising sand. Fifty dollars came from fans at a local ball game. A thousand dollars came from the Brotherhood of Friends in Spokane. The Brooklyn Dodgers not only donated players but then bought 30 of the memorial game tickets for a group of high school ballplayers who were collecting from all over the inland northwest, coincidentally, to play on July 10th in a Brooklyn Dodgers/Spokesman-Review-sponsored all-star game. Box seats for the game sold for $10 each, and Bing Crosby purchased $2,500 worth.

Other donations came from out of state. A bartender in New York sent a dollar. Two dollars came from a New Castle, Indiana barbershop, and $20.67 came from a softball game in New Haven, Connecticut. Back in Spokane, the concessionaire at the ballpark said he would turn over his proceeds from the memorial game day to the fund. And there were the special programs to be sold at the game for a dollar each as part of the fundraiser. The programs had a team photo in the middle. The photo had been taken the day of the last double-header, the day before the crash. It was eerie to see the fresh looks on the players' faces in the photograph, and know now what they did not know then.

The fundraiser organizers said that they anticipated the park would be "jammed to overflowing," with the game "attracting a full house" since "all of Spokane, sports fan or not, evidently wishes to ... contribute." Even with high ticket prices, they knew they had to add "several thousand portable seats" to the 5,000 or so seats normally available.

They stood at the gates as people poured in. In spite of the rain, the people came. Thousands turned out for the event.

It mattered to each soul that family was there, or friends, or their living mates. It mattered that they seemed to believe in something. What mattered most, though, were the promises. On everyone's lips. "We'll never forget these boys," is what the souls heard. They heard it in the grandstand. They heard it from the speakers on the field. Most of all, they heard it in the hearts of those they loved, and that loved them.

One of the speakers said what had been on everyone's mind. That these men were the kind that never gave up. "They never counted a game lost until the last of the ninth was finished," the speaker said. Nine souls collectively sighed. How many games had they won in the ninth? They thought of the game the day before, of Milt Cadinha, their pitching mate. It was enough, what he had done, to win that game for them.

Mel stood with each and every soul. "There's something that matters, us being here," he said. He patted Vic on the back, stood next to Chris. "Good work with the Kid," he told the young catcher (who had lost all he knew and ever wanted to be). He went to each Bob, each George. He found Freddie Martinez. "This is for you," he said to each one. "This is for you, and for who you are."

The souls stood in awe. In all the chaos and confusion, in all the times these past few days when they wondered what it all was for, they had not expected this. The words they heard – they were true. It was not about baseball, or Spokane, or sad stories for any day. But it was for them, who they were, what they had known, what they had been.

The program for the game showed each one of their faces and spoke of each of their strengths, what they brought to that field. The words in prayer, in remembrance, did too. And then one of the speakers spoke of their shadow forms: "Strange players come to play in your honor, but to us, your shadow shapes are there...."

And now it was complete.

There came a time when the surviving players went to stand on the field, as a sign of something good. First they called out the names of those not there: Ben Geraghty, gone home to recuperate; Dick Powers, in the hospital with a broken neck. Then they called out the names of those who were at the field, and each player stepped forward. Milt Cadinha, Joe Faria, Gus Hallbourg, Pete Barisoff, Irv Konopka, Dutch Anderson.

Then they called out one last name: "Levi – Chief! – McCormack!" And out stepped Levi. The crowd roared. Levi waved a sad wave as all the survivors stood still in the midst of the cheers. With all of them stood nine souls. In that way, the team stood together one more time.

And then it came time for the Oakland Oaks and the Seattle Rainiers to take the field. Mel looked to each of his spirit-shadow men. "They said the fans will see us out there when these men take the field," Mel said. He looked solemnly at the group of dead men, from one to the other, and then asked: "What do you think? Do we give them someone to see?"

Each looked to each other and slowly nodded assent. In one fluid motion they took to the field and found a man to stand beside, as their shadow selves. Nine men for nine souls. After all, there was one last game to play.

In the stands sat Howie Haak, Branch Rickey's right hand man. He was there for the high school all-star game, co-sponsored by The Spokesman and the Brooklyn Dodgers, to be played on July 10th. It was a scouting trick that Brooklyn used, to find all the talented kids out in the sticks. It just so happened that the bus crash had been right before the scheduled all-star game. And so it was that Howie Haak watched the crowd as they cheered, cried, and stood in the rain, while nine souls played in shadow form with some of the best and the brightest in the Pacific Northwest.

Headline: July 9, 1946: "LOYAL BASEBALL FANS POUR OUT HEARTS TO TUNE OF $50,000"
Subheadline: "Tribute Paid By 6000 At Benefit Game For Kin Of Spokane Indians"

The story attempted to describe the event. It told of how fans came from all around the area, some from great distances; how, "from Coeur d'Alene, Idaho, 600 residents came by caravan with the state patrol escorting them to Ferris field from the state line;" how rain threatened all afternoon, and the "worst began to fall" before the game started (letting up two hours before the game and resulting in a less-than-packed crowd at the stadium); how, in spite of the rain, all tickets sold; how there was a "brief but touching pre-game ceremony" before the game started; how, during the ceremony, the owner expressed his appreciation to the fans for their "wonderful co-operation and assistance during trying times;" how the umpires told the fans to tell them if the "men in blue 'missed' one" (making fans cheer at the assignment of this task); how Johnny Price, "heralded by sports writers throughout the midwest and Pacific coast as the cleverest baseball comedian in the minor leagues and perhaps in the nation, thrilled the fans with a 30-minute exhibition, undoubtedly the greatest Spokane fans have seen;" how players from old were there; how Casey Stengel and the "Oaks" played 17 of their own and most of their best; how the rain started coming down in the sixth and by the middle of the seventh it was obvious they would be unable to finish (inspiring the "hearts pour out" headline).

And yet it was the kind of event that needs no substance – where substance only distracts. And the article failed to record the most important part: that people went to that game to tell nine souls that they would always be remembered. And how could it be otherwise? We will always remember, they said from the stands.

And still the money kept coming in.   The local bus drivers' union contributed $10 while individual union members contributed $72.84. A benefit softball game in Colfax, on the same night as the Spokane fundraiser, netted about $300.

In the end, they counted all pennies from all sources. Total: $118,567.41. It was more than double the original goal.

In all those days, from start to finish, up to and including the benefit game, everyone's efforts showed. And yet, for as much as every one did in the aftermath, there was absolutely nothing that any one could do to change what had happened. This is what they knew as they sat and watched the benefit game – that there was no way to bring these men back in body form. In that, hearts could not stop pouring.

In amongst it all, nine souls shone brightly into the coming night as they stood on that field and played in the form of an echo. And as the game shut down in the seventh (as the rain poured down and everyone went running for cover), nine souls, one by one, slowly lifted away towards the evening star.

PART 5

Spark'd

After Joan of Arc had died, there was a period of time where nothing really happened. No battles were really fought; certainly no wars were won. There was stagnation, a blankness. Although her troops had floundered during the year between her capture and her death, at least they had had the hope of her rescue to keep them afloat. Once she was dead, they stood very still.

But time marched on, as time is wont to do. And when the still-would-be-king Charles' right hand switched from a weak man to a stronger one, and when that new leader began the completion of what Joan and all her generals and troops had started, those who loved Joan put on their armor and returned to the fields and fought for Charles again until France was freed from the British. It was what she would have wanted them to do.

But even as they won what she had started, they never forgot. They wished she was there, to help them. They called on her in battles, and remembered her, her bravery, her spirit, her life – the lift that infused life in them.

Then there was the Bastard. He never told anyone but La Hire that he had gone to her execution. So only La Hire and Friar Isambard knew that he had been there. But even they did not know the rest – how her voice praying to the heavens as she burned became a voice inside his head; how he knew, for the rest of his life, what it had been like for her to hear voices, since now he was never free of hers; how he kept waiting for her voice to recede; how it never did; how he was secretly glad that it never left.

He lived with her always inside his head – his heart. He wondered nearly every day for the rest of his life if he could have saved her – what if he had done this, done that... And every time he wondered, he could hear her voice telling him to rest; that there had been no other way; that he had been brave to come to her as he had... Do not weep, she would whisper in his ear. He would rub his face, where her ashes had lain, press his hands into his cheeks, eyes, so that she would always be near. It was the only way he knew to survive his feeling that he had failed her.

In the end, they all passed on, and that could have been the end. But there was something more about her story that would never die. Perhaps it was her spirit itself that made sure she would live on, beyond the lives of those who knew her well, or even knew her at all, and into the lives of those who had perhaps never heard of her, but just knew that they wanted to know what it meant to live with intent, with purpose, with a sense of a call-

ing – of a destiny – of a way to fulfill the very nature of their beings. For there can be nothing greater than to fufill the very nature of your being. In that way, and by that legacy, she would never die.

Ben Meets the Boss

Manager Ben Geraghty of the Spokane Indians held a big huddle at the Davenport yesterday with Branch Rickey, grand panjandrum of the Brooklyn baseball empire. The bossman, in Spokane as a stop in his tour of the farm chain, was accompanied by his son, Branch Jr., and his wife. They were all present at Ferris field last night as the Indians broke their own class B attendance record.

At first there were the births of babies. A girl, then a boy, then a girl. A girl named Chris, after her father. And a boy named Mel, after his father.

At some point there were marriages. Betty Lyden became Betty Timmerman. Grace Hartje became Grace Anderson, as she and Dutch, the team's trainer, became close and then married. Enough time had passed for there to be a time for marriages again. In fact, one might say that Chris Hartje had something to do with Grace and Dutch. It was, after all, Chris who lent Dutch a twenty dollar bill to help him get home to San Francisco the day of the crash. Was it Chris, in death, who urged Dutch forward to insist on paying Grace back that same twenty dollar bill? She would need it when the baby came. And maybe it was also Chris, in death, who got Dutch to give the twenty to Grace's mother when Grace refused to take it directly from him. It was the beginning of something, to be sure. It would have been a selfless act. But Christian Hartje had learned a lot about selfless acts as he helped to hold on to young Vic's soul when his own heart ached for home. Perhaps it was through these acts that he saved his own soul from being lost.

Then, there was the ending of careers. The very next off-season ended more than one career. Milt Cadinha injured his pitching arm. Faria, too, but Cadinha's career ended when he broke his arm while throwing a pitch in a winter league. And Pete Barisoff, another pitcher, survived the crash almost unscathed only to die in a fire in Los Angeles.

Jack Lohrke was the one who really went on to play, and play well. He always wore a red shirt. The next season, 1947, they wrote an article about that shirt. He never said anything about it, other than it came from the gear he got off the bus before the crash, and that he had to wear it. In the end, he stopped playing too. But he did well, in the meantime, in his red shirt.

They call him "Lucky Lohrke," from how he kept cheating fate out of taking his life in crashes (plane or bus). The record books call him that. Newspapers call him that. Sportscasters call him that, too.

If you ask him though, he'll let you know in no uncertain terms: the name's Jack.

Other changes came about. Sam Collins and the Brooklyn Dodgers signed a working agreement and, in 1947, the Indians became a full time farm team for the team that ran farm teams across the nation. Dwight Aden left the Tribe's front office, opting for insurance sales to be his full-time endeavor. His replacement was Denny Spel-lecy, news reporter and sometime sports editor for The Spokesman-Review – a man who knew baseball, the Indians, and the Brooklyn Dodgers. Ben Geraghty, healed from his wounds, got promoted to manager. Glenn Wright, the post-crash 1946 manager who had re-gained his way after the crash, made way for the new manager and became part-time trainer and travel secretary instead.

Then Levi McCormack sent back his contract unsigned.

And then he was signed.

No more Dwight, but Denny. No more Milt, but McCormack. No more Glenn, but Geraghty.

And so, while everything changed, some things remained the same. In that way, the 1947 season began.

And what a season it was.

There was the knowing how to win part of what came out of 1946.

And how could it be otherwise, when the Brooklyn Dodgers are your link?

There was a system in place, and the Indians were part of that system. The managers from all the teams were coached as one body before spring training, all the way down in Florida. Then the Dodg-ers chose the time, place and date that spring training began. They chose each team's players. It was a well-run machine, this farm system.

And still there was some independence. After all, Levi was cho-sen by Spokane, and Collins and Geraghty and Spellecy. He needs to play for us, they had said. And the Dodgers had acquiesced. It turned out that they needed McCormack, too.

That well-run machine made its way into the annals of baseball. The new team stormed the field that old teams had dominated. Fans got ready to learn new names and create new legends out of these young (oh so young) new players. And fans came in droves. More than ever, they flocked to Ferris Field. And even amongst all the new, young faces, everyone was glad to see two old, familiar ones. Levi McCormack and Ben Geraghty stood on the sidelines in amongst all that youth, ready to begin.

And then there was the part about knowing how to be a mate.

For it was in that year, 1947, business or no, that baseball became about seeing beyond the skin color of a man, as Jackie Robinson started by playing first base in Brooklyn. There was something regal, to be a part of the Dodgers as they became a part of history. Dangerous, irritating, uncertain, too – but regal most of all.

And it was in 1947 that men in Spokane – some, not all – learned about how to move beyond a static moment into movement again. Even with all the changes, there were those who remembered from the year before – who had vowed to remember always as the old future became the present and the present made room for the new future.

And it was in 1947, before the season began, even before the managers' organizational meeting that Ben attended, that Levi brought Ben out to the edge of town to stand in a parking lot out by the Spokane River, out by Old Nat Park where a baseball field's grandstand used to be, just to hit a ball or two into the river – to see how far they could hit.

By midseason, there was some question about what the "win" part really was about. For the Dodgers juggled players based on what worked for them. Did that mean Spokane would lose some of their best midseason?

Just four days from June 24th, a blow came. The newspaper reported that Spokane's outfield was getting pulled to Santa Barbara, a team less likely to win in their (lower) division. It was the way of the baseball farm chain, lamented the newspaper, complaining of how the major league teams were "notorious for strengthening low clubs at the expense of the higher brackets," and questioning the Dodgers' penchant for valuing money over the development of players. Injuries, too, plagued the Indians. Between potential theft and injuries, the Tribe was hobbled. Or was it?

For it is when logic falls to the wayside that a team can win. Perhaps it is in the freedom of the play, knowing that they only can go up from here. Or perhaps it is in the slap in the face, as some of their best and brightest get ready to be taken from the team, leaving the rest to refuse to give up, if they so choose. Perhaps, without the early failure – or even without the slap – the team does not rise to the occasion.

Perhaps without the early failure or the slap in the face, the manager would have forgotten to remember why it was he chose to come back to Spokane in the first place.

There was something about the possibility of losing his outfield in the days before June 24th that made Ben remember. Suddenly he halted for a moment. Kept his temper for a moment. Stopped drinking for a moment. Stopped running a business for a moment.

Suddenly he wanted to get back to the game.

And so it was that he turned to Levi and said he was ready. So Levi called out in his mind to another, who called out to the others – "to the River, to the River," the soul of Mel Cole called out into the atmosphere – and by the time Levi stood with Ben in the parking lot by the river, where the grandstand used to be, to hit balls into the river, their mates stood there, too. It was the eve of the anniversary of the beginning of their deaths.

"Tell me about them again," Ben said. And so Levi did. He spoke of each and every one, as best he could.

In the end, the 1947 outfield stayed. Did the Dodgers change their mind? But it didn't matter. The threat had served its purpose; the awakening already had happened. And after that, the Spokane Indians didn't say die, didn't cry uncle, didn't give up, but played to the end with effort, losing games all along, playing in moments of brilliance, scratching their way to the top after all. And missing first place by .001 percent.

Yet even in that end to the season, they had won. For they set two national attendance records, drawing a single-game Class B record of 9,438 on August 8th and breaking their own 1940 single-season mark with a total of 287,185 for the season. In that, they couldn't lose.

Within it all were moments to define the season.

There was the moment that the season began. It is always a moment when the season begins. The first pitch, the first hit. They won that game, the day the season began. It was a good omen.

Then there was the moment that George Schmees, center fielder, refused to step back into center field. A raucous argument was taking place at third base, as Ben and four players disputed a call by the ump that the runner had been safe. George Schmees had migrated into the infield from his post in center when the base umpire saw him and asked what he was doing. "Playing center field," George is reported to have answered. The ump ordered him back to his spot and George refused, "averring that he could play center field any place he chose." By the time George had turned around to obey, he was thrown out of the game by the home plate ump – a different umpire altogether! Which was when George came running in to the pitcher's mound, "gesturing wildly and impolitely." It took a "flying tackle" from another Indian to save the ump from George.

The Indians had to forfeit that game. But it was quite a sight to see.

And then there was the moment of honor. For there was a sense that filtered through the field that Levi, still not fully recovered from the bus crash, was not much longer for the game. So they held a ceremony in his honor, and in honor of the six seasons that he had played for the Tribe.

A "group of anonymous admirers" gave him a car, a "1947 Buick Roadmaster sedan, dark blue in color to match that cap that since 1939 has bobbed on the Chief's head in the outfield, around second base, or wherever he has been needed to give his ball club the necessary boost." The Nez Perce tribe, "of which he is a chief," gave him a shotgun. The team gave him matched luggage, the league gave him a gold baseball, and the fans stacked up a multitude of gifts up on the pitcher's mound. "This is one of the nicest guys that ever played baseball," owner Sam Collins said to the 7,977 in attendance.

And Levi, standing in his signature red shirt – the color of shirt he always wore – spoke beautifully of what it meant to him, to be honored in this way. "This is the most perfect night I've had in baseball," was part of what he said. "Thank you all from the bottom of my heart. It's been a pleasure to play for such wonderful fans. I hope our team will do as well in the future as we have in the past. Again, thanks."

Celebrating, drinking that beer that Ben said he would drink with him someday, dealing cards, just the two of them.... Ben's plans, on and on, going on and on... Levi leaning in, listening, though the beer clouded him, waiting to understand this moment from the next, dealing each of them a card turned down and one turned up.... Red back, red back, Jack of Diamonds (to Ben), six of clubs (to himself).

Ben let out a holler and flipped up his underneath card. "Ace of Spades!" he said triumphantly. "I win your Roadmaster!" Which was funny because they weren't even betting.

It was what Levi had been waiting for. Should they go? Should they not? Jack of Diamonds, Ace of Spades. It was time to go. So he dug his keys to that new Buick out of his pocket. "We have a place to go," he said. "Okay," Ben said, trusting Levi, grabbing the rest of the beer and the deck of cards. Off they went, to a parking lot where ball used to be played, out by the river where boys and men watched Babe Ruth play back in 1924. As they drove there, Levi called out again that night, for the second time, to Mel, who called to the others, who gathered at the riverbanks, waiting.

And that was where they all were when the sun rose in the morning. Levi stretched out, half-awake, Ben sitting, talking, Levi smiling, chuckling now and then at something Ben said.... And ghosts overhead, laughing too, helping in all the plans.

And there was a third thing. It was about being in the moment of the game.

For within days after the end of the 1947 season, for all its successes and failures, Spokane learned that there would be no more. At least there would be no more from anything they had known from 1946. Everything from that season was gone.

There was a new owner. And nothing was to stay the same.

No more Sam Collins owning the team. No more Ben Geraghty managing it. No more Levi McCormack playing within it. No more Denny Spellecy running the front office. Not even would the connection to the Brooklyn Dodgers exist. All was gone.

They headed for the river one last time. Ben was talking nonstop. Levi was nodding. They made quite a pair, the two of them did, Ben with all his talk and Levi with his ability to see what Ben wanted to create. From a distance I could see them – Levi's clear face, leaning in to hear each of Ben's words; Ben with his back to me, towel over his left shoulder, cap on backwards, head nodding, hands gesturing, stepping forward with Levi's steps, animated in his talk (I could tell, even from my view). I could see Levi's face, now and then, crease into a smile; Levi's laugh, now and then – now *that*, I could hear.

This time it was time to shake their heads in wonder at where their team had gone. New owner, new manager, new everything.

Ben would get his release, Sam had said. So would Levi. They would own their own contracts. Ben already knew he was not much longer in Spokane. He urged Levi on. "Coach," he said. "The men already look up to you. Become a coach," he said again, and Levi nodded. Maybe he would, he said in return. Maybe he would.

They sat on the edge of the river now. No more batting practice. Just in amongst the weeds on the edge of the bank. It got quiet, as Ben sat back. All of a sudden, there was not a lot for him to say.

"You come out here much?" Ben asked, after awhile.

"Some," Levi said.

"Does it do you any good?"

"Some."

They were quiet again.

"Do you talk to them still, out here?" Ben asked.

Levi nodded.

"What do you say?"

Levi sighed. He thought about it. "I say I'm sorry they're not here. I say I miss them. I say how much Herb Gorman reminds me of Bob James," he said, smiling, remembering his sense that Bob had been flattered by the comparison.

"So ...they just sit out here, waitin' for you to show up?" Ben asked, skeptical of Levi's "talking" to these men, yet wishing it to be true.

Levi shook his head no. "Just when I come," he said. "Just when I call out and say I'll be here. Sometimes they were at the ballfield too, when we played." Levi stood up to skip some stones. They were quiet for a while more.

"You think they're here?" Ben asked. "I mean, now."

Levi shrugged. Nodded. Tossed a couple more stones. One of them plunked into the water, no skipping.

"I sure hope they're here. I want someone besides me to see how bad you are at skipping stones," Ben said. Levi laughed, and kept tossing stones, skimming the surface of the water with them.

"What do you think they would say?" Ben asked. "You know, if they were here."

Levi thought about it. He looked out to the river. "Job well done," he finally said.

Ben shrugged. "I don't know that they would say *that*," he said. "We didn't win the pennant, Sam has sold the team...."

"Job well done," Levi said again. He turned to his friend with a serious look. "I'm not saying I *think* that's what they would say," he said. "It's what they *are* saying. Right now. 'Job well done,' is what I hear."

Nine souls stood as a bridge between riverbanks just a little above where the two men sat. They stood where Levi the boy would have sat (had there been a bridge there) to watch Babe Ruth, back in 1924, hit a homerun for the hometown fans. Yes, they thought, that's what we are saying. Job well done, mates.

• • •

And yet, even in the part about moving on into the next moment, there was no lack.

In 1948, even with nothing left to remember from the year or two before other than one player from 1947 – the only repeat – something happened.

For the team in 1948 became known as the team that knew how to win in the ninth. Only this time they were winning in the ninth of the season – in those last few games where it would seem that they had no chance.

And so, in that way, the 1948 players somehow figured out how to carry on the legacy of the team from before that had known how to win.

And by all accounts, it seems that 1948 team figured out how to carry on the legacy of how to be a team – how to be each other's mate – even when all else seems lost for good.

Maybe the surge at the end was inspired by a terrible, terrible thing.

On July 24, 1948 – exactly two years and one month from the Snoqualmie Pass disaster – a bus transporting a minor league team from Duluth, Minnesota crashed and burned on the side of the road.

It was a terrible crash. It was a hot crackling fire. It became the fear of the minor leagues that bus crashes were here to stay.

And yet, for as terrible as it was, there was something good in it as well. For unlike the bus crash on Snoqualmie Pass that killed nine Spokane Indian players, the Duluth team crashed in a place where people could stop and help. In that way, only five died. Not "only." For five men is five men, and no one should die like that. But more would have died had there not been people to help. In that, perhaps nine men already dead were able to make a difference. Maybe they had learned how to encourage quick action from afar.

And perhaps those deaths somehow set the 1948 Spokane Indians team into swing. For it was in the month of August that the Tribe came back, from behind, in the waning moments of the season, to pull out the wins that brought them the pennant.

Perhaps the 1948 Indians suddenly chose to remember the mates that they had never known. Or perhaps nine souls had come back once more, in a moment of the game, and had played as echoes on a field that they loved, with men who needed to remember how to desire the win and how to play as a team.

Or perhaps, just perhaps, whether people remembered or not, perhaps these men were able to assist whoever chose to strive.

Certainly these nine men inspired Ben Geraghty, who died in the early 1960s, but not before coaching Hank Aaron, who called him the best coach he had ever had. They say that Ben never slept on those bus rides across states in the middle of the night, going from one game to the next, sitting right behind the bus driver, watching him take the road at every turn, drinking a case of beer along the way, never passing out, as though his watchful eye would ensure that the bus would not, could not crash.... They say that the 1946 bus crash changed him, made him the man who looked after the young Hank Aaron, made it so that he saw each player beyond skin color and to the depths of his soul – his heart – and pulled from each one the promise held within.

And certainly these nine men lived through Levi McCormack, who died young too – too young – but who remembered through his sorrow, through his damaged hip, through his journeys to the river, through his gentle ways, as he took on the job of a Spokane post-man..... They say he held his children closer and heard each person better. No one could listen like Levi could listen – no one could treat a person like Levi could....

And yes, the men lived through Dutch Anderson, who went on to coach at University of San Francisco, where they named the press box after him and where he did in one locale what Ben Geraghty did in the minor leagues – Dutch, who had a copy of that team photo that was taken that last day before the bus crash, and who framed that photo and hung it above his television so that he saw those men, frozen in time, every time he watched a game on TV.... They live through Jack Lohrke, who kept that red shirt from his gear on the bus.... They live through Gus Hallbourg, who never did wear his jacket again (that beautiful leather jacket that his mother gave him)....

As each teammate lived, he kept alive the hearts of the men who had died. And as each teammate died, his heart became a part of the hearts of those who had gone before. And so it was for every man from that team – never to forget. That would be the easy part, per-haps, to be remembered by those who had known them – by those who would never, could never forget what happened one fateful, foggy night on June 24, 1946.

But maybe the 1948 season was a chance for these men to in-spire the play of those who did not know them too. And maybe the spirit-soul saw what they did (what they wanted to do), understood what they did (what they wanted to do), and helped them once more as they worked to inspire players who did not know them but who wanted to win. I was fading away then, so I do not know for sure. But maybe that's what happened.

Whether yes or no, this would always be true: that these men were men of the heart, giving all they knew, as they played in the moment, breathed in the grass, and stood in the sun. That they were called the Spokane Nine, and that they came from 1946. That they had known how to be a team, and they had known how to win. This is what they knew, and this is what they could give, if only asked, or allowed to be heard.

And then, it seemed, there was no more. All that could be done, had been done. At least, for now. At least, for the field where they had played in 1946.

And so it was that, on October 29, 1948, just a little more than a month after the season ended, sometime between 8:12 and 8:14 p.m., a fire started in the grandstand of the modern Ferris Field, and it burned to the ground. All that was left was charred remains. A replacement never really came in the coming years. Baseball, for all intents and purposes, was finished there.

And the core of the earth stilled its song as it waited for the next beat.

APPENDIX

Front row, left to right, are: Joe Faria, who with Milt Cadinha drove to the Coast in a private car and thus escaped the accident; George Lyden, dead; Irvin Komopka, injured; Bob Patterson, dead; Bob Kinnaman, dead; Levi McCormack, injured; Jack Lohrke, injured; Jack Lohrke, taken off the bus at Ellensburg before the accident; Fred Martinez, dead; and Bob James, dead. Rear row: Business Manager Dwight Aden; Chris Hartje, dead; Vic Picetti, dead; Pete Barisoff, injured slightly; George Risk, dead; Dick Powers, injured; Ben Geraghty, injured; Gus Hallbourg, injured; Cadinha; Manager Mel Cole, dead, and Doc Anderson, team trainer who was not on the bus. The bat boy, front center, was not with the team.

162

Biographies

Below is identifying information for each man who is in the team photograph that was taken the day before the bus crash.

Men Who Died In The Crash

Mel Cole – Mel Cole was the 25-year-old manager of the team who became manager on the eve of the season opener. He and wife Mimi purchased a home with a big basement with the plan to provide a space in their home for the players to gather after games. Mimi was pregnant with their first child at the time of the crash. Mel was from Sacramento and had played professional ball in El Paso, Texas, Joplin, Missouri, Tacoma, and Wenatchee, Washington before World War II. He served 19 months in the Navy overseas, going through the Solomon campaign before his discharge in October, 1945.

Chris Hartje – Chris Hartje was the catcher who was optioned to the Spokane nine days before the bus crash. He arrived in Spokane five days before the crash. Chris was from San Francisco. He and his wife Grace had been trying for eight years to have a baby. She was six months pregnant at the time of the crash, and flew to Seattle to be with Chris in his final hours. Chris had played with minor league clubs in Oakland, Kansas City, Montreal and Syracuse and had played nine games with the Brooklyn Dodgers in 1940, before serving with the Coast Guard during the War.

Bob James – Nicknamed Bob "Jesse" James and the "Wild Man," Bob James played right field and was tagged as an enthusiastic base runner with an easy grin. He was roommates with Jack Lohrke and Freddie Martinez. Bob was from Tempe, Arizona, and had a brother named Bill who is discussed in the novel. At the memorial game, Bob was remembered as the man who hit the ninth inning single that produced the winning run in the Indians' final game before the crash. He played in Idaho Falls in 1941, and then served in the military during World War II.

Bob Kinnaman – Bob Kinnaman was a pitcher for Spokane in 1940 and 1941, before the War. In 1941, he won 22 games for the Indians. Prior to Spokane, he played for Washington State University and in

Idaho Falls. He was a First Sergeant in the Army Corps of Engineers and served 29 months overseas in Europe during World War II. Bob pitched three games for the Oakland Oaks in 1946 before coming to Spokane. His last victory for Spokane came the night before the accident when Spokane rallied to beat Salem in the ninth inning after Bob had come in as relief pitcher.

George Lyden – George Lyden was a 22-year-old relief pitcher from Tensed, Idaho, near Tekoa. He was married to Betty. They had two young sons. George was named after Babe Ruth, whose real first name was George. He pitched his first start for the Indians on June 23, 1946, the day before the crash. He pitched all nine innings. He was considered one of the most successful relief pitchers that Spokane had. He played briefly for Spokane in 1942, before joining the Navy. During the war he was stationed in Memphis, Tennessee, where he played with the Navy ball club.

Freddie Martinez – Freddie Martinez had just been moved to the outfield at the time of the bus crash, but likely was on his way back to the infield because his roommate, Jack Lohrke, had been called up by San Diego to play there. Freddie had solid offense, batting .353 at the time of the crash. Freddie was married with a baby on the way, but was living with roommates Jack and Bob since his wife was not in Spokane. The 24-year-old was from San Diego. He served in World War II for three years, including a year and a half in the South Pacific, and was discharged from the Navy in November, 1945.

Bob Paterson – Bob Paterson was the center fielder who took over from Dwight Aden, who was known in Spokane for committing only one error in the outfield the entire time he played for the Tribe. Bob was known for being a fast runner, and led the Indians that season in runs scored as well as bases stolen. He was married to Dorothy Paterson, who was one of the three wives who wrote a thank-you letter to Spokane after the bus crash. Bob was from San Francisco. He played in Idaho Falls in 1942 before serving 38 months in the Coast Guard.

Vic Picetti – Vic Picetti was quoted as being "the most promising freshman in the Pacific Coast league in 1945," the year before the bus crash, when he played first base for the Oakland Oaks. At 18, he was the youngest of those who died from the bus crash. His father had passed away the year before. He had a fiancee, Betty Evans, and a younger brother and sister, as well as his recently widowed mother as his immediate family. The newspaper reported that the Spokane Indians team had been planning a surprise visit home for young Vic after the away-game series that they would have played had the bus made it over the pass.

George Risk – George Risk played shortstop for the Indians, although he also played in the outfield during preseason. He went to college at Pacific University in Oregon, where his former teammates instituted an award in his honor for the best ball player. He was known for carrying in his wallet three two-dollar bills with their corners torn off, for good luck. Spokane was his first year in professional baseball and was batting .348 at the time of the crash. He was known for being one of the most adept at beating out a bunt. He spent from June, 1942, to December, 1945 in service as a staff sergeant in the Army, where he played for the Army's service league in Salt Lake City, Utah.

Other Men Pictured

Dwight Aden – A Willamette University graduate, Dwight Aden was business manager for the Spokane Indians in 1946, having played for the Indians in the late 1930s and early 1940s in center field. He had a stellar career with the Indians and was the beloved center fielder before World War II, when he served in the Navy, primarily as a flight instructor. He was best known as having only one error in all his playing time in Spokane. He was business manager for the team for one year, and then switched full time to his insurance business. His wife Esther is pictured receiving a check from Bing Crosby in the amount of $2,500 as part of the 1946 fundraiser. In 2003, at the Spokane Indians' 100th anniversary celebration, Dwight Aden threw out the first pitch. He currently lives in Spokane.

Dutch Anderson – Dutch Anderson had played for the Indians in earlier seasons, but in 1946 was the team trainer. He knew Chris Hartje from San Francisco, and was from San Francisco himself. Dutch was not on the bus on June 24, 1946, because he had to go to San Francisco for one day to work at the newspaper to keep his union's license. Chris Hartje had lent him a twenty to help pay for the trip. Dutch insisted on paying back Grace Hartje that twenty dollar bill, giving it to her mother when Grace would not accept it. Dutch and Grace ultimately were married. Dutch coached at the University of San Francisco, and the USF press box was named in his honor in 2002, when he was called a "USF Coaching Legend." He also was a scout for four professional teams, including for over 20 years for the Giants. Dutch always had the photo of the entire 1946 Spokane Indians team framed above his television at home. He passed away in 2005.

Pete Barisoff – Pete Barisoff, who was 21 at the time of the accident, was a left-handed pitcher. His brother Bill played ball for the Bremerton team, which was the team that the Indians were on their way to play at the time of the bus crash. Pete was the player who was reported to have said that Vic Picetti was their best player on the team. He suffered a chipped heel in the bus accident. In 1947, he played ball at Bremerton with his brother. He is credited with saving Irv Konopka's life by dragging him out of the bus. He died in a house fire in the fall of 1947.

Milt Cadinha – Milt Cadinha was the pitcher who pitched on opening night that year. He escaped the bus crash because he and childhood friend Joe Faria had driven over to Bremerton with their wives in Joe Faria's car. It was the only time that season that they had driven to an away game in their own vehicle. He and his wife had married just before the season. He also pitched a two-hitter game on July 7, the day before the fundraiser, where he "pitched his heart with every throw," and won one of the few post-accident games that the Indians won that year. He had served in World War II in the Army Signal Corps, and was at D-Day and the Battle of the Bulge. He played semi-pro ball in the off-season in 1946, but broke his arm on a pitch. He became a long-time insurance agent in Castro Valley, California and passed away in 2002.

Joe Faria – He and Milt Cadinha were boyhood friends. With Milt, Joe avoided the bus crash because they had decided to drive over separately to Bremerton. Joe also was a pitcher. He ended up hurting his arm and quit baseball the next year to begin 39 years as owner and operator of the Stadium Club, a celebrity hangout in San Leandro, California. In 1942, he played in the Pioneer League in Twin Falls, Idaho. He passed away in 1992.

Ben Geraghty – Ben Geraghty came to Spokane after the 1946 season had started, and took over second base from Freddie Martinez. He had played before the War with both the Brooklyn Dodgers and the Boston Braves. He suffered a broken knee cap and a V-shaped cut on the top of his head. The Indians signed him on as the manager for the remainder of the 1946 season, but his doctor prohibited the job. He came back in 1947 to manage the team, and came within .001 percent of winning the league. He became an outstanding minor league manager, winning two awards as Minor League Manager of the Year. He coached a young Hank Aaron, who credits him as the best manager he ever had. He died of a heart attack in 1963 at the age of 48.

Gus Hallbourg – Gus Hallbourg came to Spokane as a newlywed and a pitcher. He was the friend of Levi McCormack who walked out of the bar that would not serve Levi alcohol because Levi was Native American. He also is the player that draped his leather jacket over Vic Picetti as they waited for the ambulance to arrive. He suffered burns on his arms and hands from the bus crash. Before the War, Gus played in Texas and California and pitched for San Diego at the end of the 1941 season. He was from Massachusetts and Rhode Island. He served in the Navy for four years. After 1946, Gus played two more seasons and then became a telephone lineman in Manteca, California, advancing to supervisor before his retirement. He currently lives in Manteca.

Jack Lohrke – Jack Lohrke played third base for the Indians, and was roommates with Bob James and Freddie Martinez, who both passed away in the bus crash. Jack was on the bus to Bremerton, but was called back to Spokane during the team's dinner stopover in Ellensburg, right before the bus crash, because San Diego had called him up to go there to play. He is the one who nearly "knocked out the play clock" on the last game before the crash. After the crash, he played all or part of seven seasons in the major leagues, and several more years in the Pacific Coast League. In 1947, he was said to always wear a red shirt that he had from his gear from that bus ride. After baseball, he became a security guard. He served in the Army infantry at Normandy during World War II. He and his wife had two sons and a daughter. He currently lives in San Jose, California.

Irv Konopka – Irv Konopka, a catcher, played football at the University of Idaho and then signed with the Spokane Indians straight from the university. He had been with Spokane for about two weeks at the time of the crash. He was trapped in his seat in the crash, but Pete Barisoff saved him by pulling him through a window. He suffered a broken shoulder and a head wound. He played baseball in Boise, Idaho, in 1947. He died of cancer in 1970.

Levi McCormack – Levi McCormack played left field for the Indians both before and after World War II. He was Native American, of the Nez Perce and Spokane tribes. Prior to playing for Spokane, he played for Seattle in 1936 in the Pacific Coast League. He grew up near the Nez Perce Reservation in Idaho. He went into the Navy in 1942, and served nine months in the South Pacific. He is considered one of the best-loved Indians' players ever. He suffered a broken nose and a hip injury in the bus crash. He stopped playing with the Indians after 1947 (though he played semi-pro ball for several years). He married after baseball, and he and his wife had three sons and four daughters. He tried private business, then became a Spokane postman. He died suddenly in 1974.

Dick Powers – Dick Powers pitched for the Spokane Indians in 1946. He was from Oakland, California and spent most of his career associated with Sacramento. He suffered a fractured skull and a broken back. It took nearly two years for him to recover. He didn't play ball again. He spent ten years in the wholesale meat business and then went into real estate, all in Oakland.

Bat Boy Ken Benshoof – Ken Benshoof was not on the bus on June 24, 1946, because he could not find Dwight Aden the night before to get permission to take the road trip with the team. He was 14 at the time. He played basketball and baseball in high school. He played Legion ball and semi-pro ball, and went one year to Willamette University on a basketball and baseball scholarship. He transferred and then graduated from Eastern Washington University. He was a member of the Navy reserves, served two years active duty, remained active in the reserves, and retired as a Navy Captain. He married in college, and he and his wife have four children. He spent 37 years with Hallmark Cards in sales and marketing in Portland, Oregon. He currently lives in Redmond, Oregon.

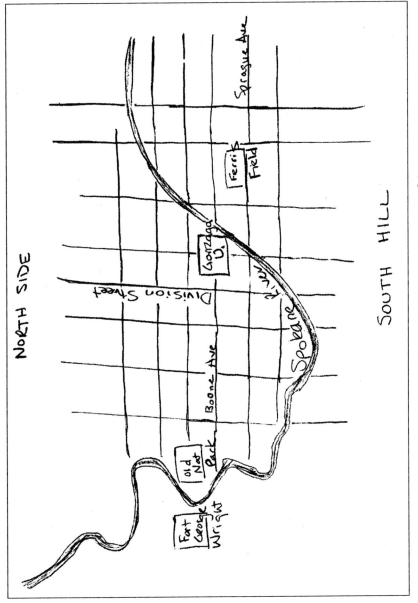

Map of Spokane, Washington (not to scale)

Afterword

This is fiction, and only based on a true story. I have tried to be true to the facts while necessarily creating from my imagination most of the scenes and possibilities. I write this Afterword to explain my process.

In researching the facts, I made a copy of every newspaper article I could find from the local newspaper. I spoke extensively with Jim Price, local sports historian in Spokane and news columnist who is writing a book on the history of the Spokane Indians baseball team and who has over the years interviewed many of those whose lives were directly affected by the bus crash. I also talked to the Indians' front office, though their information from 1946 is limited. I went to the local museum and looked through all the materials there, including an original program of the memorial game. I turned the 60-year-old pages of the program oh so carefully, so there was no chance for them to tear. I met with people from that time who are still living, to see what they remembered of the accident. I asked numerous survivors – both players and widows – to read drafts of what I had written. I tried to find family members of all the players who died.

Some facts didn't surface until later drafts, after I had a chance to talk to people who could tell me things that had never been written down. Examples are Levi's ouster from the bar because he was a Native American; George Lyden being named after Babe Ruth; Gus Hallbourg's jacket, and his draping it over Vic Picetti; his telephone call to his wife Roberta, right before she received a phone call from the team; the Picetti family's anxiety-filled night while awaiting news; Grace Hartje nee Anderson's early morning phone call of the crash; her running to the street in her nightgown to see the newspaper headlines; the twenty dollars Dutch Anderson gave her mother to repay his debt to Chris.

Some facts in early drafts ended up being wrong. For instance, in one of my first drafts, Chris Hartje had two stepsons. This came as quite a surprise to Grace and her two daughters (though her daughters did say that they always had wanted a brother or two). Other facts were incomplete. I did not learn until recently, for instance, that Vic Picetti's father passed away in 1945, and the resulting circumstances there.

Some facts undoubtedly will surface after the book comes out. I did try to locate family members for all the players, as well as all survivors, but I didn't always succeed. I will try to keep readers updated through my website of any factual corrections.

Certain scenes come from two or three sentences that I read in news articles. For instance, there was only one mention that I found about the Coles' home. It was in a short article written after the crash that explained that Mrs. Cole was selling the home that they had bought with a big basement for friends. From that notation, I built the scenes around the house. I confirmed those scenes later when I learned that there had been a housing shortage for the players, and after I drove by the house as it stands today. Another example: there is one article in 1947 about Jack Lohrke wearing a red shirt as a rookie in the major leagues. The report indicates that he would say nothing about the shirt except that it came from the bus. The rest of what I say comes from my imagination.

Some scenes, in addition to the ethereal ones, come *only* from my imagination. For example: did Levi McCormack see Babe Ruth play ball in 1924? I don't know. I like to think so. Certainly we know that Babe Ruth played here in 1924, and that boys hung off that left field fence to watch. We know that Levi lived near Spokane at the time, and was a boy who loved baseball. But we can't know if he came that day to watch.

Another question: did Levi hit nine balls from the parking lot into the river, or streak his face with tears? I do not know, although I think it is consistent with what I have heard about Levi. People have told me how Levi was a good man who was a little scary for some and who had a heart of gold when you got to know him. They have told me that he had this way of listening to you as if you were the only person in the room; that he took seriously his Native American heritage; and that he was famous in this town long after his playing days were over. A colleague of mine who grew up in Spokane told me that, as a child, he believed that Levi was the best ball player that ever lived, and that no one could have convinced him otherwise. That is the effect that Levi had on people. But we'll never know for sure if he hit balls out of Old Nat Park that night.

I also tried to stay alert to things happening around me that could give me ideas of how to write the book. An example: I had been pondering the relationship between Ben Geraghty and Levi McCormack, and was trying to get a grip on the quality of their friendship. In the midst of this, I went to a pow wow in Post Falls,

Idaho. Before the actual dancing, there was a round-up of sorts of all dancers and their friends and family. I glanced up at one point and saw two men, one Indian, one white, in front of me. The Native American was a fancy-dress contestant, and so was all decked out in feathers and colors. He was stunningly beautiful and tall and looked like the photos I have seen of Levi. I could see the side of his face as he listened intently to his friend. His friend was not a contestant and so was dressed in jeans and a T-shirt. He had a baseball cap on backwards and a towel over his shoulder. He was speaking animatedly, non-stop. I watched as the two men continued moving around the arena and out of my sight. My attention then turned to another dancer, another outfit....

A few minutes later, I glanced up and I saw this pair walking past me again. I happened to look up at the same angle as before, as they were just beyond where I was sitting, so that, again, I could only see the side of the dance contestant's face as he listened intently to his friend with the backwards baseball cap who continued to talk nonstop. I again looked away as they circled out of my sight.

A few minutes later, I looked back up. There they were again, at the exact same angle as before. This time I saw the Native American man throw back his head a little and laugh. I heard him too. I thought, oh my gosh, there is something for me to see here. And that's how I came up with that one scene towards the end of the novel, with Levi and Ben walking out by the river in the early morning hours, with Ben sharing his plans for the future. The image came full circle when, months later, the first posed head shot that I was ever given of Ben Geraghty was one where he is wearing his cap on backwards.

The parts about Joan of Arc (discussed in the Foreword as well) are also based on significant research, but include a strong dose of my own imagination. Both her trials and her ultimate vindication a few years later were transcribed back in the 1400s, so her story is one of those rare historical events that is extremely well documented. I have reviewed parts of those writings. I also read Mark Twain's novel, The Personal Recollections of Joan of Arc, which gave me a sense not just about what she did, but also of who she really was. It is from my imagination, however, that I write about the General (the Bastard of Orleans) appearing before her as she readies to die. Logic brings me there. I know he tried to rescue her. How could he have chosen to stay away on the day of her death?

People have asked me how I chose to write this novel. It was in the summer of 2003 that I learned of this story. At the time I had worked on my own ancestry, and with a couple of groups in anniversary years on their histories, always with an eye towards seeing where the unhealed wounds may still exist. As a lawyer, I am drawn to conflict that needs resolution, so it would make sense that I would help in that particular area.

In the midst of this work, I learned that the Spokane Indians minor league team was celebrating its 100th anniversary that summer. I thought that perhaps there could be work that I could do with that organization, and I bought a video called "100 Years Of Spokane Indians Baseball" to see if there were any times of crisis for the team (since that was my specialty). And that is how I learned of the bus crash. In the end, there was not a project for me to do for the baseball team itself. But by then I was hooked by this story of these men. They were such incredible men, such men of heart. I couldn't walk away from the story. I remember talking to Jim Price, my sports historian friend here in Spokane, and telling him that I thought I was going to write this novel. I can't seem to get these guys out of my head, I told him. Jim just nodded. He knew exactly what I meant. So that's how the novel came to be.

I have been told by some people who lived back then, and who knew these men, that I am accurate in describing them. I did try. I read articles over and over. I talked to people who knew. I sat with the story for months on end, drafting and editing. I wanted to be accurate in my sense of these men, because that is what it ultimately takes – capturing a sense of something and hoping it holds truth. To be told that I "got" a lot right is a high compliment. For those who think that I have gotten things wrong, however, I do ask that readers remember: this is a fictional book.

Acknowledgements

So many people have helped me in the writing of this book. First and foremost, I must thank those who survived the bus crash – players, widows, family members, children not yet born at the time – for reading the manuscript and for re-living the details of this immensely personal tragedy so that I could do the best by this story as I could. In particular I thank Dwight Aden, Grace Anderson and her daughters, Ken Benshoof, Gus and Berta Hallbourg, Betty King, the Lydons, Mel MacArthur, and Anne McCormack for adding personal stories to the details of what I already had, and for helping this story come to life. Enormous thanks also goes to sports historian and writer Jim Price, who dedicated so much time to educating me on the details and the flavor of what he knew about what happened in 1946. Because of Jim, I was able to impose on families as little as possible. Also to Jim I owe thanks for a meticulous reading of the transcript.

A very special thanks goes to Milton Kahn, the best publicist ever. I am so grateful to have him on this project.

Thanks also to the entire team at AuthorHouse, for the quick and professional work and suggestions, and for talking among themselves and with me about how interesting they think the book is.

Thank you also to the various folks who helped me put this book together at various points along the way. Tony Bamonte volunteered his publisher's expertise by reading an earlier draft and giving me publishing advice; Larry Reisnaur, at The Spokesman-Review, worked beyond the call to ensure that the images for the book were the best possible; Mark Mohr, creator of the video "100 Years of Spokane Baseball," volunteered his information and provided additional photographs so I knew what to look for; Ann Colford helped create consistency of text; Michele Mokrey took her artistry and our friendship and produced a wonderful portrait of me; and Kurt Schmierer of Washington Digital and Photo, Marcia Smith, and Tim Schwering put great effort into ensuring a high-quality final product. Organizations helped as well. Thank you to the Spokane Libraries, for keeping wonderful records; to the Northwest Museum of Arts and Culture of Spokane, for having a beautiful library of photographs; and to various folks throughout the Pacific Northwest who helped in other research endeavors.

I am immensely grateful to my group of friends who have supported me throughout this project, and who have read through so many drafts, including the initial drafts that were very different from the final outcome. Thank you all for all that you have done, and for believing in me. Although I do not name you individually, please know that I am so grateful for your help and support. Special thanks goes to Jennifer and Jerry King, for inviting me over often for wonderful, home-cooked meals, and ensuring that I did not become too reclusive during the writing of this book.

And then, of course, there is my family. Thank you all so much. To my parents, for believing in me and believing in this project. I could not have done this without you. To my siblings, for being there in an instant whenever I asked for help. To my other relatives, for your enthusiasm for my writing, and to my uncles, for reading earlier drafts of the book. A special acknowledgement goes to my nieces and nephews. In each and every one of you, I see the promise of the future.

Finally, I thank all those who have already gone. Thank you to the 1946 newspaper reporters who recorded what happened; to the people who tried to do the best they could when this tragedy struck; and to the baseball players themselves, for being the kind of men whose story should be told. We should always remember you.

About the Author

Beth Bollinger is a literature major turned lawyer. She was born in Wisconsin in 1961, and grew up in California and Arizona. She lived abroad in England and Japan, and spent a year in Wyoming as a news reporter before moving to Washington, D.C., for law school. Beth moved to Spokane, Washington in 1994 to work at the federal public defender's office and presumed that she would return to the "other Washington" after completing her two-year contract. Instead she stayed in Spokane, opened up her own law practice, and started writing.

Beth is the co-author of the first edition of "Keys To Career Success," a community college textbook on choosing careers. "Until The End Of The Ninth" is her first novel.

Visit Beth's website at www.untiltheendoftheninth.com.

Printed in the United States
50589LVS00006B/157-759

9 781425 936655